****

LIVING IN THE SEVENTH DAY

****

A Novel by
Bestselling Author

Jeanetta Britt

This is a work of fiction.
The events described here are imaginary;
the settings and characters are fictitious and not intended to represent
specific places or persons, real or imagined.

Inquiries should be addressed to J. Britt
(brittbooks@msn.com)
Twelve Stones Publishing LLC
P. O. Box 921, Eufaula, AL 36072-0921
www.jbrittbooks.com

Library of Congress Control Number: 2014915058
ISBN 978-0692300503

Printed in the United States
First Edition

Editor: Fairrene Carter-Frost
Glorias G. Dixon
Margaret Wilson
Cover: Michelle Stimpson

Scriptures from *The Holy Bible*
King James Version

Other Books by the Author
JEANETTA BRITT

Exciting Novels

W.O.O.F. (Women of Overcoming Faith) (ISBN 978-0-9712363-8-7)
Empty Envelope (ISBN 978-0-9712363-5-6)
The Lottie Series:
    Pickin' Ground (Book 1)   (ISBN 0-9712363-3-x)
    In Due Season (Book 2)   (ISBN 0-9712363-4-8)
    Lottie (Book 3)   (ISBN 0-9712363-6-4)

(E-Books are also available for Kindle and Nook.)

Inspiring Poetry

Flittin' & Flyin' (ISBN 978-0-9712363-9-4)
Under the Influence--Spoken Praise (ISBN 0-9712363-7-2)
The Trilogy:
    Poems from the Fast   (ISBN 0-9712363-0-5)
    Reunion   (ISBN 0-9712363-1-3)
    Third Ear   (ISBN 0-9712363-2-1)

Visit Jeanetta online:
www.jbrittbooks.com
www.Facebook.com/Jeanetta Britt
www.Facebok.com/@JBrittBooks
www.Twitter.com/@JBrittBooks

FULL BLOOM

I set my life under the feet of others
And they flattened me to the floor
Like a flower that had been stepped on
They set me outside the door.

But the Lord stepped in and claimed me
Brought me back into the room
And little by little He's restoring me
Bringing my life to full bloom.

Acknowledgments

It is such a blessing to be able to trust and rest in Jesus. And it is a pleasure to share this writing experience with fellow believers. Many thanks to my terrific editors, Glorias Dixon, Fairrene Carter-Frost, and Margaret Wilson. Thank you, Glorias, for not pulling any punches to make this story as believable and enjoyable as possible. Thank you, Fairrene, for lending your critical eye to make this an easy read. And thanks to you, Margaret, for always keeping it real! Michelle Stimpson, national bestselling author and ebook guru par excellence, thank you so much for being willing to share your expertise with all of us—writers and readers, alike. Your calm patience and gentle way make you the perfect mentor.

Many thanks to all of my social media friends for your kind interest, for getting the word out through sharing your posts and tweets, and for taking the time to write such terrific reviews. And thanks to my many readers, encouragers and prayer partners for sharing your 'like precious faith' as we continue on our journey—together—to give Him glory! Your love and support mean so much.

Friends for a lifetime…Sisters & Brothers Forever!

CHAPTER 1
Meeting in the Airport

"Uggh!" Cristal Richardson shot up from her uncomfortable seat, wedged in between two other women, and shook her cellphone like a piggy bank. Her voice was swallowed up by the noisy crowd of disturbed passengers in Concourse C at the Hartsfield-Jackson Atlanta International Airport. In fact, there was a near-mob scene on every concourse because all flights had been cancelled due to the treacherous weather conditions sweeping the south. The delay had crippled every flight since noon, and for several hours stranded passengers had been swarming the gates like packs of chaotic zombies, with no end in sight.

"Ladies and gentlemen!" A tense voice with a decidedly southern accent crackled over the airport intercom. "May I have your attention, please?" The bubbling caldron of steaming passengers simmered down to a low boil. "The airport appreciates your patience while we deal with this unforeseen weather emergency." The voice gained altitude. "All flights are on hold due to gale-forced winds and near zero visibility caused by Hurricane Allee. This killer storm's been brewing down in the Gulf for nearly six days, and we were expecting it to maybe hit us tomorrow. But it's taken a crazy turn, and it's barreling down on us today…uhh…but no need to panic. The latest Doppler radar reports indicate the winds are moving off to our north and east, and we may be able to resume some flights over the next few hours." The voice wobbled in for a landing. "So, we're asking everyone just to sit tight while we ride out this storm, and we'll keep you updated periodically on its progress. Please be sure to check the monitors when flights resume because gate assignments may change due to the delay. Again, thank you for your patience."

The announcement did not fall on deaf ears because everyone in Concourse C had witnessed the fear-stricken faces of the seventy or so passengers who scrambled off of Flight 425 from New Orleans—the last plane to land before the airport was buttoned up tight. The host of assorted strangers clung to each other, gasping for air and slinging tears, as they hurled themselves up the ramp to safety. It was clear they'd formed unbreakable bonds while being slammed around by the terrifying elements. They huddled together on the floor in a tight circle and spoke only to each other in monotones and fearful whispers.

Comprehending the severity of the situation, others began to follow suit. A number of standing passengers shrank to the floor, curling up on backpacks in dusty corners. They snuggled their loved ones close to their hearts, realizing this was a threat they'd have to survive together. When the social media sites leaked the news that Hurricane Allee had shattered and hurled plate glass windows in Concourse A, it triggered another swift exit. This time, passengers fled the window seats, like a shot had been fired from the starting pistol at a 40-yard dash. The squeals were deafening.

"Uggh!" Cristal repeated more quietly this time, shaking her gold-trimmed handheld. "This phone is deader than a doornail!"

The two women seated next to her raised vague eyes from the screens of their own handheld devices and looked right through her.

"Now, how will I get in touch with that worrisome man of mine?" Cristal reclaimed her seat, persisting in her monologue.

Jasmine Davis, the older woman at her left elbow, had a crop of unkempt natural hair shot through with wild strands of gray. She raised her tired, brown eyes and pointed to her right. "There's a console with outlets over there, young lady," she said.

"I know that." Cristal batted her thick lashes for emphasis. They graced gorgeous, wide grey eyes set under carefully arched brows. Her grey eyes, which she inherited from her mother's side of the family, were all the more dazzling, contrasted against her deep mocha skin, which she did not. "But I packed my charger in my checked luggage." She smoothed her mahogany weave, which hung to her shoulders, with her diamond-encrusted left hand. "Who knew, right?"

Leeza Manchester, the svelte, well-dressed blonde with the swan neck and liquid blue eyes at her right elbow, blew out a breath and peered up again. The bangs on her fashionable pageboy, set against her pale, porcelain complexion and gleaming gold accessories, gave her a retro-Twiggy look. She was beginning to hate she'd ever sat next to these two chatty women, although hers had been the last seat in the house. An elderly gentleman had vacated it just for her, and she wasn't about to give it up. "If it will help at all," she offered in a tight-lipped Manhattan accent, "I have a universal charger you may try."

Cristal scooted around to give the woman a long, solid look, not sure if she was trying to be smart or helpful. Totally out of options, though, she said, "All righty, then, I guess it's worth a try. 'Cause you see I'm from the ATL, and I need to let my husband know I'm all right or he'll be back out here, bad weather or no bad weather, to take his baby home." She rose again, and every nearby eye swept over her killer figure. She was about 5'-8" without an ounce of unwanted fat and a tight, round butt that got plenty of notice. "But I ain't going home." She wiggled her gold skinny jeans into place. "I'm getting on this plane if it's the last thing I do."

"Then, o-kay." Leeza fended off her wordy intrusion. "Here's the charger. Hope it helps." She turned up her nose and added, "Over there."

Cristal took the charger from her creamy white hand and gave her another long, hard look. "Say, you ain't trying to be—"

"Nice." Jasmine edged in, smiling under her breath as Miss Thang met Miss Vain. But she figured this young white woman might need to watch her step around an agitated Miss Thang. Besides, with the thunder booming overhead, tensions in the cramped quarters were mounting like a powder keg; and she didn't want this pair of salt-and-pepper divas to set off the fuse.

"I beg your pardon?" Leeza flashed at Jasmine, fighting back the urge to be rude.

"Sharing your charger." Jasmine smiled sweetly. "That was real nice of you."

"Yeah…nice," Cristal said, just this side of a bad attitude. She swiveled on her four-inch heels and switched off in the direction of the console; her arms swinging like she was attacking life with a hatchet.

"Not a problem." Leeza re-posted her 'Do Not Disturb' pose and continued to scan her screen for incoming texts.

"Look at that." Jasmine pointed to a young man with sagging pants and hat turned backwards helping an elderly woman lift her heavy bags. "Two people with seemingly nothing in common, but it seems we all get a little closer at times like these, when tragedy strikes," Jasmine said as lightening pierced the sky and the fierce rain hammered the wall of plate glass windows in Concourse C.

"I'm a New Yorker." Leeza mumbled, recalling the events of 9-11. "The worst of times can bring out the best in us," she said, without looking up from her screen.

"I'm Jasmine." The older lady persisted. "Jasmine Davis." She smoothed the sleeve of her pea-green pantsuit and toyed with the tiny gold cross at her neck. "I guess we might as well get acquainted; seems we're going to be here awhile."

Leeza eyed her computer screen once again and shrugged. She really wanted to get back to work, but the swell of agitated passengers and these irritating women was making it hard to concentrate. "Well, okay." She set a half-smile on her elegant face. "I'm Leeza. Leeza Manchester."

"Where're you headed on this frightful day, Leeza?" Jasmine said quietly.

Leeza let out a strained sigh. As a Junior Account Executive with Bradford & Baker, Inc., one of the most prestigious advertising and marketing firms in New York City, she traveled over 75% of the time, all over the globe, in fact. And she had one hard and fast rule— she did not divulge her destination to fellow travelers. Given the nature of her cut-throat business, she never knew when one of them might be a hungry competitor snapping at her heels. And being under 30 and single, she also took every precaution for her own personal safety. So she generally stayed away from needless associations. But there was something disarming about this harmless-looking woman with the gentle smile that reminded her of her dearly departed grandmother. So she caved. "Okay. You go first." Leeza conceded. "Where're you headed…Jasmine?"

"This trip is kind of a downer for me." Jasmine admitted. "I just dropped my daughter off for the first time at college—freshman, Howard University, Washington, D.C."

"Oh, I see." Leeza nodded consolingly. "Empty nest syndrome starting to kick in, huh?"

"Yeah, something like that," Jasmine said. "And, now, I'm headed back home to Dallas."

"Well, I travel…a lot." Leeza confided. "I was in Beijing, China just two weeks ago." She smiled at the memory of her successful trip. "Just left Key West, Florida." She continued. "And, now, I'm on my way to Nashville to clean up some marketing nightmare that our client has created over at the Grand Ole Opry."

"Wow! That must be interesting work." Jasmine exclaimed. "I wanted to travel once, but I've got my family, you see." She smiled weakly. "But circling the globe like that, don't you ever get dizzy? Forget where you are?"

Leeza chuckled in spite of herself. "Well, to be honest," she said, "I have this little trick. I always leave a message on my phone before I go to bed to remind me where I am the next day." It sounded a little silly hearing it in her own ears.

"That is a neat trick." Jasmine giggled. "But even that probably wouldn't help me."

"Why're y'all grinning?" Cristal burst back on the scene holding up her phone in victory. "Your phone cord worked, Girl." She shoved it back into Leeza's hand. "And I've quieted my man down for the time being." She glanced over her shoulder. "But them folk back there are plenty scared this wind's gonna peel off this roof like a pop-top can. They—"

Jasmine and Leeza sealed their lips and swept her away with an icy glance. Cristal reclaimed her seat between them, but their chilly reception gave her the distinct impression that she'd been the source of their amusement. Their dismissive attitude struck a nerve in her as raw as the lightning that lashed out against the defenseless sky. It reminded Cristal of how her mother and her sister made her feel. Like them, these two women acted like they somehow *out-classed* her; and she wasn't having it.

"So...*Miss Universal Phone Cord*." Cristal spouted, launching the first attack in her own defense. "Where's yo man?"

Leeza gasped, taken aback by her directness. She didn't know whether to answer or run away from this lunatic. But she was determined not to back down, so she shot back with all the swagger she could muster. "I have a career. I don't need a man."

Cristal smiled slyly. "Quick on yo feet, huh? I like that." She snorted. "Besides, Girl, it's none o' my business. I'm just messing with ya." She swiveled toward Jasmine and fired her second missile. "And you don't get off that easy, Missy." She looked down at her solid gold wedding band. "Where's yo man?"

Jasmine gave her the evil eye to put her in check. "What's your name, young lady?"

"Cristal." She spouted, without skipping a beat. "Cristal Richardson. Pronounced like the champagne." She fluttered her grey eyes. "My Mama knows a whole lot about high-priced thangs."

"Well, Cristal," Jasmine said, taking the time to pronounce it correctly. "I'm Jasmine Davis, and this is Leeza Manchester. She travels all over the world for her company."

"Now, ain't that special." Cristal twinkled. "But that don't get you off the hook."

"What?" Jasmine frowned, getting fed-up with her audacity.

Cristal glanced down at her wedding finger again. "Where's yo man, Girl? The question is still on the floor."

Leeza couldn't help giggling under her breath. *She's a hoot.* But she didn't dare say a word.

Jasmine pursed her lips. "I'm headed home to my *man*...in Dallas."

"Now, that wasn't so hard, was it?" Cristal said, exploring the expression on her face. "So why're you looking like a woman who ain't quite sure—"

"Jasmine's daughter just went off to college in D.C." Leeza jumped to her aid.

"That's nice," Cristal said slowly, letting the other matter drop for the moment. "Real nice."

"And where're you headed?" Leeza pressed the point, wondering how she'd gotten pulled into this madness. *Am I really playing referee between these two women I don't know...and don't care to know?*

"Oh, it's kind of a long story." Cristal admitted, lowering her guard.

"We've got time," Jasmine said sourly, happy to shift the spotlight her way.

"You see," Cristal whispered, "I want a baby. Real Bad! And I've screwed that man o' mine upside down and sideways. So if that didn't get it, we need to see what medical science has to offer." She shrugged. "'Cause God want us to be fruitful and multiply.' Now, ain't that right, Jasmine?" She shifted toward her. "I saw you reading yo Bible on yo tablet."

"Yes." Jasmine held the device close to her ample chest. "But perhaps, dear, some situations require us to just pray and wait."

"What you say 'bout that, Leeza?" Cristal turned for her opinion.

"Not a subject I can address," Leeza said uncomfortably. "I'm not religious."

"Now, one thing my husband is, y'all, is a praying man," Cristal said, pulling them into her confidence. "And if all that praying ain't getting it, we'd better get on with the program—'cause 'Faith without works is dead.'" She smirked. "Don't it say that in the Bible, Jasmine?"

"Yes, but I'm not sure that scripture applies here." Jasmine fingered her cross.

Leeza rubbed her temples, trying to figure some way to head off the conversation since she was land-locked between these two worrisome women. "So...where're you off to, Cristal?" Leeza blurted. It was as plain-vanilla as she could come up with in a moment's notice.

"Oh, I'm sorry." Cristal giggled self-consciously. "I didn't say, did I?"

"No, you did not," Jasmine said, still sounding a little miffed, but making an effort to let bygones be bygones.

"I'm going to the Houghington Clinic in Houston, Texas," Cristal said. "They have this wonderful, new experimental program down there to help couples just like us who're having trouble getting pregnant."

"But doesn't your husband have to go with you for something like that?" Leeza said, sounding genuinely concerned.

"Well, it probably would be best." Cristal admitted. "But I'm having the hardest time getting it through that thick skull of his that we need to do something different." She blew a stray hair out of her eyes. "Didn't somebody famous say, 'If you keep on doing the same thing, you keep on getting the same results'...or something like that?" Her voice bobbled.

"But don't you and your husband have to be on one accord?" Jasmine frowned.

"You don't get it do you, Jas-mine?" Cristal drew out her name like she was a third grader. "That man will do whatever I say. I'm just going down there to that clinic to get my facts straight, and then I'll get him on board." She crossed her grey eyes at Jasmine. "You're married. Don't you know how it works?"

A shadow fell over Jasmine's face, and she quickly tried to conceal it. She settled for saying, "Well, if you say so."

"What's up with you, Married Lady?" Cristal folded her arms across her luscious cleavage. "You act like you don't have yo man in check. Is that it?"

Jasmine's back tensed. "I've never thought of my husband as someone to *have in check.*" Her eyes rimmed with hot tears. "I'd settle for...a good relationship."

"Ladies." Leeza sang out. "Maybe we should take this discussion down a notch. People are beginning to stare."

Cristal and Jasmine looked around self-consciously at the other passengers whose seats backed theirs, and the ones packed across the aisle whose eyes were glued in their direction. They were craving something juicy to take their minds off the raging winds and the flashing light show that was piercing the dark, angry sky.

"I just get so excited." Cristal lowered her volume. "I've wanted this for such a long time. Years!" Her eyes flamed. "I'm 30-plus."

9

She smoothed her hair. "Leeza, you're probably not as old as me, but haven't you ever wanted anything?" And unable to resist the urge to needle her one more time, she added, "Or do you have everything a girl could want…you and yo job?"

"Sure." Leeza admitted warily. "I want things." She quickly scanned a text coming in on her handheld. "I want a promotion on my job," she said. "I deserve a promotion on my job. But women in corporate America don't always get what they deserve." She doubled down on her emotions and pressed her spine against the dull green chair. "Ever hear of the glass ceiling?"

"Yeah, I've heard of it." Cristal yawned. "But I still don't get it. Black women have always had to take care of themselves—"

"It's not always a color thing." Jasmine chimed in.

"Not at all." Leeza welcomed the chance to display her liberal point of view. "It's when you should be able to go higher in your chosen profession, but you don't, because factors beyond your control get in your way, which shouldn't be there in the first place."

"Like what?" Cristal snapped.

"Like men!" Leeza seethed. "The good ole boys who know all the angles to get ahead and won't share them with you. Or better yet, use them to block you."

"It's not always men," Jasmine said. "Sometimes it's the lack of education or training—"

"Don't you believe it!" Leeza felt her temperature rising. "I have a Bachelor's from Yale and a Master's from Harvard. Is that enough education for you?" Leeza blew out a sharp breath and slowed her pace. "My Dad saw to my education. He didn't spare any expense, because he's always wanted me to be a professional success. And he didn't want my being a woman to stand in my way."

"Well, at least you don't have the added iss-ue of being black." Cristal inserted.

Jasmine cut her a stern eye. "Everything is not about black and white. There are a lot of other factors keeping women down—"

"Like greedy men." Leeza reiterated.

"And conniving women." Jasmine added for good measure.

"Well, my mother never worked a day in her life." Cristal glossed her perfect French manicure. "But she could get anything she wanted outta my Daddy. So I guess she busted that glass ceiling wide open, huh?"

"Some women want to do it on their own." Leeza snapped.

"Well, more power to 'em!" Cristal drawled. "But I'd rather do it the old fashioned way…let the man do the heavy lifting."

"But there's no guarantee he'll stay—" Jasmine's words slipped out before she could pull them back.

Cristal's eyes scrolled over Jasmine again. *The woman ain't even…50. Plump, but pleasin'. Bet she was straight-up eye-candy at 20…humph…guess these last 25 ain't been so kind. Pretty brown skin sagging…acting all old…looking like she 'bout to cry. What's up with that?*

"What?" Jasmine bristled as she caught Cristal eyeing her.

"Oh, nothing," Cristal said. "I was just wondering why yo husband didn't come with you to drop yo baby off at college?" She tried to mask her burning curiosity under her sugary tone. "Is he home with the rest of the kids?"

"No." Jasmine shifted uneasily. "Madeline is our only daughter."

"Well, then, why didn't he come?" Cristal whined.

"His work." Jasmine averted her intense stare. "Dex is lead attorney at Grantham & Granger, and he couldn't find the time to get away."

"Uh-huh."

"Wow!" Leeza exclaimed, attempting to steer the conversation off the rocks. "Going off to college. I remember those days. Lots of fun!"

But Cristal wouldn't let it go. "So did you call yo husband and tell him you got caught up in a hurricane out here all by yourself?"

"Texted him." Jasmine said primly.

"And did he call you back?"

"Why should he?" Jasmine's brown eyes blazed.

"Don't cover for yo husband." Cristal snapped.

"Ladies." Leeza whispered again, motioning to the backs of their closest neighbors who appeared to be all ears. "Can we dial this down a bit?"

"No!" Jasmine carped. "You let her tell me; why should he call?"

"'Cause he gives a care; that's why!" Cristal's hands rose in exasperation.

"So…" Leeza tugged on the wheel again. "Has Madeline decided on a major?"

"Art History." Jasmine offered with a weak smile. "Although her daddy's deathly opposed to it; says you can't make any money at that."

"Sounds like my Dad," Leeza said softly.

"How so?"

"I've had a passion for art since I was a kid." Leeza smiled. "And when I'm really stressed, I still paint to relax…and I've been painting a lot lately."

"What'cha paint?"

"Watercolors, mostly, some oil on canvas…landscapes, angels…whatever pops into my head." Leeza grimaced. "But like your husband, my Dad wouldn't hear of it. He wanted me to get into a profession that would support my lifestyle, whether I marry or not."

"I guess that's understandable," Cristal said, "but at some point you've gotta do *what* you love…or *who* you love." She winked. "By the way, did yo daddy call you?"

"Call me?" Leeza looked stunned, thinking she'd headed off this line of questioning.

"About the bad weather, I mean." Cristal chirped.

"No." Leeza frowned. "Why should he?"

"Well, did yo job call?" Cristal persisted.

"No." Leeza's blue eyes bobbled, unable to steer around her penetrating logic.

Cristal raised her brows. "So you're running around all over the world…for a company that won't give you yo due…and a daddy who's pimping you…but they don't even call to check on you in a hurricane?"

"That's uncalled for!" Leeza blared. She was really beginning to resent this crude stranger who seemed to be able to cram into a nutshell all of her growing frustrations about her high-paced career and her dad, who was pushing it down her throat. "They trust my ability to handle my own affairs." Leeza huffed.

"Okay, *Miss I'm-married-to-my-job*." Cristal fired back. "As long as you get the job done for *them*, do you think they even give a flying leap about what happens to *you*?"

"So what do you do?" Jasmine leveled Cristal with a cold stare. "You seem to know something about everything."

"Me?" Cristal pointed to herself with a cock-sure grin. "I'm having the babies in the family, like my Mother did; and like my big sister, who has four already." She twirled her finger. "My husband, Malik, does the work. He owns his own funeral home here in the ATL, and he makes big bucks 'cause folk be dying every day."

"Money's not everything." Jasmine snipped.

"Oh, yeah," Cristal said without missing a beat. "Well, whatever's next is a looong way off."

"And what do you do, Jasmine?" Leeza overlooked Cristal. "Besides escorting your daughter to college, I mean?"

"I'm a PRN," Jasmine said.

13

"Wow!" Cristal blew a low whistle, ignoring Leeza's attempt to freeze her out. "Big Bank! Mucho Dinero! Cha-Ching!"

Leeza couldn't resist smiling at Cristal's wild antics. "What? I don't get it," she said.

"This lady's a registered nurse with a license to write her own check." Cristal snickered.

"I don't know about all that." Jasmine smiled sheepishly. "But it does allow me to pick my own assignments and give as much time to my family as I need."

"See what I mean." Cristal blew smoke off her imaginary pistol. "License to kill old bank accounts in a single bound! She strips 'em before my husband plants 'em."

"Do you work for an agency or on your own?" Leeza explored.

"I have my own clients." Jasmine relaxed her defenses. She enjoyed them taking an interest in her work. "Some of the larger hospitals in the area, and then I have some private clients, as well."

"Rich, *old* private clients, huh?" Cristal glimmered.

"Some." Jasmine pursed her lips, but she couldn't hold back a grin. She was beginning to warm up to Cristal and her sharp wit, which had a way of penetrating to the heart of a matter. "But it is a very rewarding career."

"Yes, sounds *very* rewarding." Leeza giggled.

"See, ladies!" Cristal grinned right along with them. "That's all I've been trying to say—"

"What?"

"I figured the two of y'all have some important careers...and I don't—"

"We never said—"

"But I do have one thing." Cristal waved her gold-edged phone. "I have somebody on the other end of this line who cares if I get blown away by this monster storm. And having somebody who cares...that's important, too."

"You're right, Cristal." Jasmine agreed. "It is very important."

"Uh-huh." Leeza glanced down at another incoming text.

"That's it!" Cristal clicked open her phone. "Give me yo digits."

"Ahh—" Leeza hesitated.

"Don't worry." Cristal grinned. "I'm no stalker. I ain't got that kinda time."

"So—"

"Give me yo numbers, ladies."

"But why—"

"Because...we all need somebody...and I wanna be yo somebody who cares." Cristal firmed. "Besides, look at them." She pointed to the huddled passengers from Flight 425. "There's gotta be a mighty good reason we've all been squeezed in here together like this today—"

"But I do better with texts." Leeza argued.

"And I'll certainly add both of you to our prayer list." Jasmine smoothed her hand over her cross.

"Looks to me like y'all got enough cyber buddies and prayer partners to last a lifetime." Cristal appealed with her hands. "A text can't hear you! You need some real people to talk to from time to time. And I don't mean like church folk, who'll judge you and spread yo business around." She flashed a knowing eye in Jasmine's direction. "You ain't gotta worry 'bout me. You can tell Cristal all...'cause I ain't got no dog in yo hunt."

"But—"

"And when I call to check on you...and it won't be often...you'd better answer." Cristal worked her neck and twirled her shiny index finger. "Or else, I'll sic my bloodhounds on you to see if you're really all right. Got me?"

"Yes, but—"

"But-nothing." Cristal shook her phone. "C'mon. Give."

"O-kay." They groaned.

Cristal logged their cell numbers into her phone—first, Jasmine's; then, Leeza's. "See." Her gray eyes smiled prettily. "That wasn't so hard, now, was it?"

"Ladies and gentlemen, may I have your attention?" The excited southern drawl boomed over the airport intercom again. Everyone rose to their feet in rapt anticipation. "We have good news! The crippling winds are moving off to our east; the rain is letting up some; and the fog is lifting. All northbound and westbound flights are being rescheduled immediately. All eastbound and southbound flights will be made available as soon as possible." The voice whirled. "Be sure to check the monitors for your flight information and gate assignments. We expect all flights to be back on schedule over the next several hours. Thank you for your patience."

"Yay! Yippee!" A wave of hugs and cheers went up in Concourse C. Everyone scrambled for the monitors.

CHAPTER 2
Jasmine

At the stroke of midnight on Saturday morning, Jasmine Davis drug her suitcase up the steep walkway of her 5,000 square foot Colonial from the Yellow Taxi she'd taken from the Dallas/Fort Worth International Airport. She was exhausted from the long layover in Atlanta, due to Hurricane Allee, and the equally long flight. She felt tired and heavy, and older than her years. Her pea-green pantsuit was a rumpled mess. Her natural hairdo was more frazzled than usual. And every nerve in her body was tingling with exhaustion. She had texted her husband, Dex, when she finally boarded the plane in Atlanta in hopes he'd meet her flight when it touched down in Dallas. But Dex was a no-show. So instead of risking an interminable wait in the misting rain, Jasmine grabbed a cab home. The ride to Plano, a north Dallas suburb, was nearly 30 miles.

The front porch light was off when she arrived. Jasmine rang the doorbell in the off-chance she wouldn't have to rummage through her purse for her keys. But there was no answer. She propped her luggage against one of the graceful, white columns set across her expansive front porch and fished out her key ring. With one tired shoulder, she pushed open the solid mahogany front door with its impressive bronze footplate; and with the other, she rolled her heavy bag into the massive foyer.

The house was completely dark. Jasmine disarmed the state-of-the-art alarm system and switched on lights from the foyer to the great room, making her way into her well-appointed kitchen. She turned on her sleek, chrome coffee maker and plopped down on the nearest black leather stool at her pearl-gray granite counter. She didn't bother to call Dex. She couldn't bear to hear another one of his excuses, or leave another unanswered message. Sitting at the counter in the kitchen she'd planned so meticulously for her family's enjoyment, Jasmine's mind raced back to the last conversation she'd had with Dex. It had been in this very room before she and Madeline had left for D.C.

***

"So what do you want from me?" Dex's voice reeked with annoyance.

"What're you saying, Dex?" Jasmine cried. "I only want what every wife wants from her husband."

"You're not every wife, Jasmine." He swaged his muscular, six-foot frame; his brown skin smooth as hot molasses. "And I'm not every husband. I thought you knew that by now."

"But I can never count on you, Dex."

"Never say never," Dex said flatly. "You depend on me plenty to pay all the bills around here." He swiveled his arms around the sprawling kitchen. "And, now, there's private college tuition to boot! And what do I get out of the deal?" He answered his own question. "A wife who nags me at every turn about everything!"

Jasmine's face flushed hot. "But where were you last night, Dex…all night? Don't I have a right to know?"

"Sure, you have a right to know." Dex flashed his deep brown eyes on her and pushed his hands through his handsome waves. The dimple on his right cheek had lost its shine. "And I told you where I was. I was at work, finishing up the Dunston brief. We go to trial next week, and the man is fighting for his life. He's accused of first degree murder. That could get him the needle." He huffed. "I'm trying to save his future and make more money for your stuff. But you don't like my answer!"

Jasmine waved her hand in defeat, like she'd done so many times before. She could never win the war-of-words with her husband. After all, he was a litigator. He talked for a living. "All right, Dex," she said, afraid to push the point with Madeline waiting upstairs. "Let's just leave it at that." She headed for the staircase, thoughts raging. *'Cause what's the use of mentioning that sweet perfume you're reeking of? A different brand than last time—true—but neither of which are mine. No doubt, you'll have an answer for that, too, Mr. Lawyer-Man.*

Jasmine stopped when she reached the stairs. "I'm helping Madeline pack," she said without turning to face him. "We leave tomorrow, so I'd better get to it." Her voice cracked. "But in the future, Dex, please do me the courtesy of calling…if you're going to be working late…so I won't worry."

"Sure thing, Hon," Dex rang out as he turned up the volume on the TV. "I'll text you."

***

And, now, it's after midnight. Jasmine's mind raced as she propped her heavy head atop her shiny counter. *He knows I'm back in town. And he's missing in action…again.* She shook her head and took another deep draw from her coffee mug. She'd need at least two stiff cups of the stuff just to make it upstairs to face their empty bedroom. And, now, without Madeline, the totality of their empty nest was almost more than her heart could bear. Jasmine sighed, and the mournful sound echoed throughout all the hollow spaces. *All I've ever tried to do is keep my family together…and look at us now. We're further apart than ever.* Familiar hot tears stung the back of her eyes. *Lord, please help me!*

CHAPTER 3
Leeza

Leeza Manchester took a taxi straight from LaGuardia Airport to her office in the 80's on Manhattan's Upper West Side. The horrors of Hurricane Allee, notwithstanding, her trip to Nashville had been marginal at best. She could barely understand those yammering yokels; much less make sense of the mess they'd made of her perfectly scripted advertising campaign. She'd tried to set them back on course, but she'd gotten a horrific headache in the process, trying to decipher their lingo. *Is that even considered English?* She rubbed her temples. *Nice people, but those twangs and drawls are even worse than that...Cristal woman...who murdered the English language at the Atlanta airport. I guess she was just a preview of coming attractions.*

Leeza smiled at the thought, happy to be securely ensconced back in the Big Apple; the city she loved. She loved the tall buildings, the blaring horns, the sights, the sounds. Leeza even loved the smell of crunchy-coated pralines and Sabrett hot dogs roasting on street corners, but she wouldn't be caught dead eating any of that stuff. She drew comfort in knowing that there were as many distinct stories as there were pairs of eyes on the bustling sidewalks—locked and loaded, straight ahead, rhythmic syncopation. Insulated by the herd, she had no need to get in touch with her own feelings. Her anonymity wrapped around her like a warm blanket, making her feel deliciously safe. As she drew closer to her building, she was reassured by the sterling, block letters that reached high to the sky for all the world to see—Bradford & Baker, Inc. *Home!*

Leeza was met at the elevator by her colleague, Kyle Leary. "It's about time you got here," he buzzed. "The boss is nearly frantic." Red-headed Kyle was a self-proclaimed corporate ninja, and since they shared the same title and same boss, Leeza was always a little suspicious of his motives.

"Why?" Leeza pulled her carry-on onto the elevator floor. "What happened?"

Kyle pushed the button for the 66th floor. Bradford & Baker's advertising and marketing syndicate housed the top ten floors in the Rushmore Building. Their client list was a virtual Who's Who of Wall Street—giants in manufacturing and retail, as well as, celebrity entertainers. If you've heard of them, Bradford & Baker represented them.

"Our boss has been called on the carpet by his boss, Mr. Baker." Kyle went straight for her jugular. "I think it's about what happened down in Nashville."

"But I got that straight." Leeza retorted. "What is it now?"

"It may just be bad timing. I'm not sure." Kyle shrugged. "I think Baker and that Grand-Ole-Opry yahoo have some kind of personal connection. And maybe he jammed up our boss before you got things ironed out." He glued his eyes on the elevator control panel. "But Cole wants to hear everything from your own lips before he meets with Mr. Baker."

"Okay-Okay." Leeza frowned

Kyle lowered his voice. "You know, our boss is in line for partner again…but so is Skinner. And Skinner is brown-nosing with Baker every chance he gets, trying to beat out our boss for the slot."

"But our boss reports to Baker." Leeza's brow knitted. "Skinner reports to Bradford."

"Doesn't matter."

"But our boss should be a shoe-in." Leeza insisted. "Mr. Cole has banked thousands more billable hours than Skinner. And he's worked our butts off to do it."

"Know that." Kyle swept his eyes over the crowding elevator and moved in closer to Leeza. "But Skinner's got an edge over our boss," he whispered.

"What?" Leeza mouthed. "What could mean more than bringing in the business?"

"Are you kidding?" Kyle hissed. "Don't you know the real deal?"

"What?" Leeza nudged him.

"Skinner's assistant, Brandi Mason." Kyle scanned the packed elevator again for prying eyes and listening ears. He wanted plausible deniability if anybody overheard this conversation. He buzzed the words out of the side of his mouth. "Brandi Mason is sleeping with one of the partners—"

"Who?" Leeza's eyes swept the side of his face.

"Bradford." Kyle mouthed.

"Wow!" Leeza's mouth dropped. "Skinner's boss? The lead partner?"

"None other." Kyle hissed.

"So what's in it for her?" Leeza eyed him.

"Whatcha think?" Kyle looked queasy. "She wants your job…or mine."

Leeza moved in closer. "But she's already a Junior Account Exec, just like us," she whispered.

"Not the job we have now, silly." Kyle squeezed between clenched teeth. "The job we could get if our boss, Mr. Cole, gets promoted to partner."

"But Brandi reports to Skinner?"

"Doesn't matter." Kyle crooked his neck. "One of us could get the promotion—"

"To Senior Account Exec?"

"Yeah, no matter whether it's Cole or Skinner who gets the partnership." Kyle squeaked. "So Brandi is sleeping around with Bradford to make sure it's her."

"And Skinner's condoning this!" Leeza rustled, barely able to contain herself. "His boss?"

"Sure." Kyle elbowed the guy next to him to gain some extra inches. "Skinner would do anything to get his name on the faceplate of this building." He rumbled. "And I think the only person in the company that hasn't caught wind of it is our boss."

"Poor, Mr. Cole; head to the grindstone."

"Easier to get it chopped off, my dear." Kyle smiled wickedly.

"You haven't told him?" Leeza pinned him with her eyes.

"Nope. It could go either way, and I don't want to be *that* guy."

The elevator door opened on the 66th floor. Leeza pulled her bag out and turned to Kyle who persisted in a low growl. "I probably shouldn't be telling you this," he said. "But I figure between us, it's 'let the best man win.' But that Brandi chick…she's a skank…and I'll do everything in my power to tank her worthless butt!"

"Let's talk about it later," Leeza said. "Better go see what Mr. Cole needs right now."

"Sure thing." Red-headed Kyle drove his hands into his pants pockets. He was a little closer to 30 than Leeza; tall, slim, and pretty good looking in a suit.

CHAPTER 4
Cristal

The car was eerily quiet as Cristal Richardson left the Atlanta airport parking lot with her husband, Malik, behind the wheel. "I'm sure glad you're home, Babe." Malik chanced to break the silence.

"Uh-huh." Cristal grunted.

Malik put his strong hand on her firm thigh. Cristal shifted away from him and leaned her head on the cool window in his black, 700 series Mercedes.

"It's going to be okay," Malik said in his gentle bass. "Really, Sweetie, no matter what happens, it's going to be okay. I love you."

Cristal slid his hand off her thigh and curled up in a small ball in the passenger seat. She pulled the hood of her mink parka over her head.

"Say something...please, Babe." Malik's handsome features firmed. He was slightly shorter than Cristal in her four-inch heels, but his thick, muscular frame left no doubt that he stood his ground.

"It's like you say," Cristal said, barely in a whisper. "It's gonna be all right."

"So tell me what happened in Houston?" Malik was encouraged to hear her voice for the first time. She'd been silent since he met her in baggage claim. "What did they say at that clinic to upset you so?"

Cristal breathed nosily and straightened up in her seat. She took another long breath and leveled her grey eyes on her husband's strong, chiseled profile. "They said, 'No-way-Jose.' They said, 'No babies-R-us.' That's what they said." She shrank back into her seat.

"But how can they know for sure, Cris. They only saw you for a few hours. What do they know?"

"You're right." Cristal snapped. "They coulda had a better chance of reviewing our case, if you'd gone with me to the Houghington Clinic in Houston, Texas."

"Babe, I told you. I'm tired of clinics. I'm tired of looking to doctors to tell us what to do." Malik squeezed the steering wheel to steel his resolve. "I'm looking to God."

"Yeah. And how's that working for ya?" Cristal burned.

"Don't talk like that, Babe. You know for yourself Pastor Gabe has been praying for us, the Men's Ministry, the Women's Ministry—"

"And—"

"And there's no telling what will happen." Malik's bass rumbled. "Is there anything too hard for God? Didn't he do it for Abraham and Sarah; didn't he do it for Elkanah and Hannah—"

"My name is Cristal." She smarted.

"And God can do it for Malik and Cristal, too." He wrapped her cold hand into his warm one.

"Whatever." Cristal sighed. "I'm just tired, Malik. Take me home…please."

"Did you call your mother?" Malik persisted.

"Yes." Cristal rolled her eyes. "I called her back when I was on my way to Houston in that big ole hurricane—"

"Well, she called you back."

"She did?" Cristal bounced up straighter in her seat and flipped off her hoodie. "At the house?"

"Yep." Malik smiled, encouraged to see his wife beginning to thaw.

"What'd she say?"

"She wants us to come over for dinner…tonight."

"Tonight!" Cristal smiled. "What's up—"

"She knew you'd be coming home today, and she wanted us to come over and have dinner with her. Your sister, her husband and the kids will be there, too."

"Wonder what's up?" Cristal said hopefully. "Ain't this September? I usually don't get no invitation from her 'til the holidays."

"But she knew you were coming home today, so maybe your mom just wants to see her daughter." Malik smiled.

Cristal stared out the window. "You know," she said, "Chanel gets invited over there all the time."

"It's probably not your sister she wants to see, but her kids—" Malik cut himself short, wishing he could bite off his tongue.

"I guess if we had some kids," Cristal said faintly, "my Mother would invite me over more often, too, huh?"

"Don't think like that, Babe." Malik soothed. "Let's just go over there tonight and try to have a good time, okay?"

"All right." Cristal drew up closer to Malik and kissed him on his fine cheek. "Whatever you say, Babe. I'm just happy to be home with you." She cooed.

CHAPTER 5
Jasmine

Jasmine awoke around 10 a.m. Saturday morning when she heard her husband's baby blue Bentley pull into their four-car garage. Her luggage was tossed in the corner of their expansive bedroom. She hadn't had the energy to mess with it when she got home from the airport at midnight. She had closed her blackout drapes so she wouldn't have to endure another sunrise alone. She just wanted to sleep and not have to face the inevitable blow-up when her husband came dragging home. She tried not to care; she'd had plenty of practice at missing him. But she found it impossible to simply accept that she and Dex lived virtually separate lives; and night after night, she had to find a way to fall asleep alone.

"You're back!" Dex said smartly when he peeked into their bedroom. "And awake." He flashed a perfect smile and the dimple in his right cheek lit up. "That's quite a feat for you on a Saturday morning, isn't it?"

But his silky, smooth voice rubbed Jasmine the wrong way. It felt like sandpaper on an open wound. "What do you care?" Jasmine heard herself say. "I know you got my text. Why didn't you pick me up at the airport...or was that just too much to ask, Dex?"

"Oh, here we go again." Dex rubbed his hand through his dark waves. He had a dusting of gray in his sideburns that made him look even more distinguished—and seductive. "I didn't text you back because I knew my answer would be, no. And I knew it would upset you." He threw up his hands. "Like with everything else I do."

"I'm not upset." Jasmine's nostrils flared, in spite of her best attempt to keep her cool. "But I haven't seen my husband in nearly a week, and I'm tired of being left alone...always alone."

"Well, I'm tired of working myself into an early grave, too, but do you hear me complaining?" Dex stiffened. "Nope. I accept what I've been given, and I make the best of it."

"And you're saying, I don't?"

"I did not say that."

"You inferred it." Jasmine's voice swelled.

"I've had a long night." Dex turned to leave their bedroom. "And I expect an equally busy day. So if all you have for me is gripes and groans, I might as well get on with it."

"D-e-x." Jasmine pleaded. "Don't run away again. Let's sit down and settle this thing."

"There's nothing to settle—"

"There is!" Jasmine seethed. "You didn't even ask me about Madeline?"

"I've talked to Madi, several times." Dex exclaimed. "I always keep in contact with my Baby-Girl. We don't need you to be our go-between."

"It's just that I thought we'd have more time together once Madeline went off to college."

"What made you think that?" Dex roared.

"Alice, one of the ladies in my Bible Study, when her son went off to college, she bragged about being on an extended honeymoon with her husband."

"That's what you get for listening to the fairy tales from those old biddies you pal around with."

"They're not old biddies." Jasmine defended. "I think Alice is even younger than me."

"Then that's why." Dex retorted.

"Why, what?" Jasmine steamed.

"Look." Dex pressed his broad shoulders against the door jam. "As I see it, my Baby-Girl being away means I have more time to myself...to do the things I need to do to get my career back on track." He extended his hands. "Don't you get it, Jasmine? If I play my cards right, I could be up for partner next year. And that would help all of us."

"Unbelievable!" Jasmine scoffed. "After all you've put them through?"

"They knew that girl was lying on me." Dex's teeth clenched. "They paid her off. Case closed."

"But this is how it started before—"

"I've excelled in my work for over 20 years." Dex preened like a peacock. "They know my value to the firm. They've put that unfortunate episode behind us. Why can't you?"

"So where were you last night?" Jasmine jumped out of bed, her natural locks standing on end; the gray strands minding their own business. "You weren't here. Who were you with?"

"I don't know how many times I can say this." Dex blew out a steaming breath. "I work. Sometimes, I work late. I either sleep on the couch in my office, or go to my club and shower. Sometimes both." He snarled. "My office is in downtown Dallas, well over an hour's drive from here, and I do not have the time to crisscross the Metroplex just to hear your list of complaints." He clapped his hands together. "So that's it. I'm out o' here. See you when I see you."

"Dexter!" Jasmine called after him. "Dex, we need to talk about the holidays—" But she could hear him slamming doors from the second floor to the garage. Then she heard the unmistakable roar of his engine. And he was gone…again.

CHAPTER 6
Leeza

The secretary buzzed Leeza into her boss' office, and she stepped into his world. His floor to ceiling windows gave him an unobstructed view of the Manhattan skyline. The corner office was a reflection of his straightforward personality—a study in straight lines and predictable angles. The minimalist design was anchored by a lavish mahogany desk on one side, and a life-sized statue of a crystal flying eagle on the other. Richard Cole had one wife and two children, and their faces were displayed in suitable frames in likely places adjacent to his telephone, which was neatly tucked away on a mahogany credenza behind him. Some of the most lucrative deals for the company had been struck across his impressive desktop. But, now, it was empty, save for a lone manila folder alongside his stained coffee mug.

"You wanted to see me, Mr. Cole?" Leeza approached him reluctantly, not wanting to admit she'd gotten the message from her archenemy, Kyle.

Dick Cole leaned back in the commanding leather chair at his desk. He was a squat man with a balding head and sagging jowls. In his late 50's, what was left of his auburn strands was tinged with grey and combed straight back; except for a single strand on the top of his head, which marched to the beat of a different drummer. The decidedly green pallor of his skin, probably brought on by too much coffee and too much worry, earned him the nickname, *Toad E. Frog*, from his back-stabbing colleagues.

Cole removed his horn-rimmed glasses and drilled Leeza with his beady, eagle eyes. "Hello, Miss Manchester," he said firmly. "Close the door. Take a seat."

Leeza followed his instructions, setting her laptop case next to the chair he offered. "How're you, sir?" She ventured.

"What's this I've been hearing from Nashville, Leeza?" He snarled.

"I don't understand, sir." She shifted. "I left Nashville just this morning, and everything was fine. What are you hearing?"

"My good friend down there tells me you had everything pretty fouled up—"

"That's not the case, Mr. Cole." Leeza withstood the challenge. "I left specific instructions how to carry out the ad campaign after we kicked it off, with a complete list of scheduled tasks." She fumbled for her computer. "I have it right here, if you'd like to take a look."

"No. That's not necessary." Cole waved his hand. "As it turns out, my colleague was just pulling my leg." He wheezed a hoarse chuckle. "I may have over-reacted because he got one of the partners all riled up—"

"Mr. Baker?"

"Yes, my boss, Phillip Baker," Cole said, taking liberties with the use of a first name rarely uttered on these sacred floors. "And we really can't afford that right now." He glared.

"Yes, sir."

"As you may know." Cole lowered his voice conspiratorially. "I'm in the race for partner."

"Yes. I heard." Leeza leaned forward to bridge the distance between them.

"And my chances are very good, it seems."

"Congratulations, sir—"

"Not so fast." Cole pulled her up short. "The decision will not be made until March of next year, and there's still too much time for me to consider it a lock."

"I understand." Leeza nodded.

"Our team—you, me, Kyle—have got to row this boat as one man and keep ourselves on course until the decision is final in March. Is that clear?"

"Yes, sir." Leeza clipped.

"Your work has been exemplary until now, but we've got to step it up a notch if I'm to beat out my stiff competition—Dan Skinner."

"Yes, I know." Leeza gleamed.

"He's a squiggly cuss that Skinner." Cole took a long draw from his lukewarm coffee. "Always has been. Hard to figure his next move. But there're no dirty tricks he won't pull to get this promotion; you know that?"

Leeza thought back to her discussion with Kyle about Brandi Mason sleeping with Skinner's boss to improve his chances, and she nodded. "Yes, sir, I think he would do just about anything to beat you out."

"Good!" Cole snapped. "We must be on our toes at all times."

"Yes, sir." Leeza encouraged.

"We've got to hit him where it hurts…in his soft underbelly…his weak spot." Cole's jowls flapped.

"Which is?" Leeza's eyes rounded.

"The bottom line!" Cole steamed. "He may think he's slicker than me—smooth talking, likeable, good looking—but I've got the advantage."

Leeza's brows spiked. "Sir?"

"I know this business inside out, and I bring home the bacon!" Cole bristled.

"Yes, sir, you do." Leeza agreed.

"And that's how we're going to beat the socks off that Skinner." Cole raised himself to full height and marched around his desk like a little Napoleon. "We're going to take it to him with both barrels over the next six months."

"Yes, sir!" Leeza nodded like an enthusiastic soldier.

Cole reclaimed his seat and opened his manila folder. "Your mission, Miss Manchester, will be to bring in at least three—" He held up three fingers on his right hand.

"Three, sir?" Leeza parroted.

"No less than three, new, blue-chip clients from across the globe." He slapped the file with the palm of his right hand. "Clients that this company does not currently serve—giants in industry; luminaries in entertainment. Zillionaires!" His eagle eyes gleamed.

"Three…in six months?" Leeza mouthed.

"I've combed the globe." Cole reseated his glasses. "And I've put together this secret list of top-flight potential clients."

"Secret list?" Leeza tore her eyes away from the wayward strand atop his bald dome and glued them on the folder.

Cole gripped the folder in his greedy hands. "This is my ace in the hole—a list of twenty-five star clients we can go after, and go after hard." Cole's breath came in short, choppy bursts.

"I see, sir." Leeza said, trying not to notice his face, flashing red like a thermometer.

"Yes, this is the bombshell that will blow ole Skinner out of the water." Cole clutched the folder tighter. "And I sincerely believe if we can pull this off, Bradford & Baker will have no choice but to make me, Richard *Dick* Cole, their new partner."

"Wonderful!" Leeza smiled prettily.

"And, of course, there'll be something in it for you, Miss Manchester." Cole beamed.

"Oh?" Leeza prodded.

"If you can bring in three, new blue-chip clients over the next six months and I get this coveted promotion, I will insist on your being promoted to my old job."

"Senior Account Executive?"

"Precisely!"

"Sounds like a wonderful opportunity," Leeza said, poignantly aware of the phenomenal amount of work it would require to pull it off.

"It is a wonderful opportunity!" Cole exclaimed. "And I assure you, Miss Manchester, if you hold up your end of the bargain, and bring me three, new mega clients." He held up three fingers like a Boy Scout. "I will hold up mine. My vacated Senior Account Executive slot will be yours. I promise."

"It's worth a try." Leeza nodded.

"It's worth more than a try, Miss Manchester!" Cole banged his file. "This is life and death!"

"So, let's get started." Leeza rubbed her temples. The enormity of the workload was already beginning to give her a headache.

"Go back to your office. Clear your calendar." Cole ordered. "And meet me back here in the morning, 7:00 a.m. sharp. Then we'll go over my list of super clients, and you can have your pick of the litter." Cole locked his precious folder away in his desk drawer, kissed the key and pocketed it.

"Fine." Leeza smoothed down her blonde pageboy and gathered up her things.

"Working together, Miss Manchester." Cole bellowed as she reached the door. "We will pull this off!"

***

By the time Leeza reached her windowless office, the phone on her cluttered desk was jumping off the hook. She jerked up the receiver. "Leeza Manchester."

"Don't sound so official." Her dad laughed on the other end. "It's just your dear-ole dad."

"Sorry, Dad." Leeza smiled. "Just getting back to town and everything's in panic mode around here."

"No problem, Sweet-Girl," her dad said. "I just called to say, hi, and catch up a bit."

"Dad, I can't right now," Leeza said guiltily. "Way too much action. I'll come out there and see you on Sunday, all right? We can have a nice visit."

"Sounds good to me." Lee Manchester wheezed. "That's if you don't mind coming all the way out to Chestnut Hill."

"Don't worry, Dad." Leeza teased. "I've been all the way to China; I guess I can find my way home to Philly."

"That's my girl." Her dad's cough rattled. "That's my girl."

"Take care of yourself, Dad."

***

No sooner than she'd cradled the phone, Kyle stuck his head around Leeza's office door. "Got a minute?" he said.

"Sure." Leeza nodded. "Come in; grab a chair."

"So…did you get the boss calmed down?"

"About that Nashville thing?" Leeza frowned.

"Yeah."

"Like you figured, it was all a hoax." She leaned across her desk and gave Kyle a serious look. "And absolutely nothing can get the boss calmed down right now."

"Pretty jazzed up about this partnership thing, huh?"

"I'd say!" Leeza eyed his clear plastic cup. "Got you drinking the hard stuff?"

"Nope. Apple juice." Kyle drained the cup. "Got a stash in my office. Want some?"

"No way." Leeza made a face. "Hate the stuff."

"Apple juice? What's with you; misspent childhood?"

"Always hated it. Me and my Dad." Leeza grimaced. "Growing up, my Mom was the only one who'd touch the stuff. She'd have a slice of cheese toast and a glass of that syrupy concoction every morning I can remember."

"Your loss, my gain." Kyle crushed his empty cup and two-pointed it into her trash can. "So…did Cole set you off on a quest?"

Leeza tensed, not sure how much to divulge to her self-proclaimed rival. "Why?" She frowned. "Did he send you off on one?"

"Remember what I told you, Leeza." Kyle smirked. "I'm going to play fair with you, because I believe our true enemy is that heartless tart in Skinner's office, Brandi Mason."

"Go on," Leeza said warily.

"So I'm willing to tell you what Cole told me, if you'll tell me what he told you."

"Show me yours, and I'll show you mine?" Leeza twinkled.

"Something like that." Kyle carped. "This is a cut-throat business, for sure, but you've got to form some strategic alliances, or you'll be an island unto yourself."

"And we know what happens to loners in our business." Leeza agreed.

Kyle made a cutting sign across his throat. "My point, exactly!" He got up and locked her door.

"Then you go first." Leeza urged.

"Okay." Kyle shrugged. "While you were away, Cole called me into his office. We had a heart-to-heart."

"What about?"

"He told me my mission was to help him make partner." Kyle lowered his voice and peeked at the door. "He wants me to reel-in three, new blue-chip clients in the next six months."

Leeza released a low chuckle. "Whew! That's the exact same thing he told me, no more than 10 minutes ago."

"Geez." Kyle whistled. "Is the old buzzard competing us against each other or what?"

"So what carrot did he wave under your nose?" Leeza set her elbows on her desk.

"Boss said if I can bring him three, new blue chippers—off his secret list—he'll back me for promotion to his old job."

"Senior Account Executive?" Leeza's head snapped.

"Yep."

"That's the exact same promise he made me." Leeza scowled.

"So he is pitting us against each other…like gladiators."

"Did he think we wouldn't know?" Leeza bristled.

"I don't think he cares if we know." Kyle grinned.

"So it's winner take all, huh?" Leeza eyed him.

"Wonder what happens to the loser?" Kyle's voice cracked.

"Off with his…or her head, I guess." Leeza grimaced.

"Rotten deal all around." Kyle sagged into her office chair.

"You're telling me." Leeza moaned.

"But you have great credentials, Leeza. You've got Harvard and Yale on your sheet. You could get a job anywhere." Kyle's eyes fogged. "Me, I barely got out of college; and I barely snagged this job." Kyle Leary had grown up in a traditional Irish-American family in Queens, and he'd worked hard to drop the accent and the baggage. It was reasonable to assume one of his ancestors had also dropped the '*O*' in O'Leary for that very same reason. He'd attended City College in the day when he had money, and at night when he didn't. His dad had been a sergeant in the NYPD and his grandfather before him, both killed in the line of duty. Kyle had fought every step of the way to get to Main Street, and he'd made it.

"But you've got lots of savvy and spunk." Leeza encouraged. "That's how you got here, and that's how you've held on."

"So I guess this means war?" Kyle swaggered. "Between you and me, I mean?"

"I hate to think of it like that," Leeza said, "but I guess we have no choice."

Kyle pushed up from the chair to put some distance between them. "Like I said, I've got my eyes on that Brandi Mason." He signaled with a two-finger jab. "I'd hate for us to go toe-to-toe, only to have her sneak in through the back door."

"And like you said." Leeza reminded him. "Between us, it's 'let the best man...or woman...win.'"

"But just so we're clear," Kyle said, glaring at her from across the room. "I'm going to do everything in my power to make sure the winner is me."

Leeza's blue eyes moistened under his fierce gaze. "Okay, Kyle." Her back stiffened as he opened her door to leave. "Fair warning."

CHAPTER 7
Cristal

Straight from the airport, Malik slid his black, 700 series Mercedes up the sparkling white cobble-stoned driveway that led to the Tudor-style mansion a mile off the main road. The stately edifice was guarded by a platoon of sturdy pines and flanked by bubbling fountains, and manicured shrubs. In the growing darkness, all of the exterior lights were beginning to twinkle like fireflies.

"Cristal, dear, come in." Chantilly Moore greeted her youngest daughter at the front door of her elegant home in the Buckhead section of Atlanta—air kisses, both cheeks. She was dressed in a regal, purple chiffon caftan and gold harem slippers. Chantilly was 60 plus, but as long as there was Botox and Clairol, she wasn't about to show it. Her makeup was flawless; her hairdo sleek. The hair color of the month was Sassy Cinnamon to match the curls on her sandy-headed grandchildren.

"Hello, Malik." Chantilly flowed an elegant hand toward her guestroom. "Be a dear and hang your jackets in the usual place."

"Okay." Malik adhered to her request.

"Your sister and her family are here already." Chantilly informed Cristal. "Come into the great room. Manfred has laid out some tasty hors d'oeuvres to whet our appetites for his special dinner."

"Manfred?" Malik muttered, bringing up the rear.

"Yes, dear, my new caterer." Chantilly boasted. "I was thinking of using him at Thanksgiving, so this will give us a chance to sample what he can do."

"Well, hello, Cristal." Chanel sauntered over when her sister entered the room. "Don't you look...special?" They faux kissed as well.

Malik and Denver, Chanel's husband, clasped hands like brothers and shook vigorously. "Good to see you, man," Malik said and sealed their greeting with a snap. Malik was slightly taller and sturdier in build. Denver's claim to fame was his movie star good looks, and kinky red hair. His light-colored skin was speckled with freckles on his cheeks and hands. Denver made eye contact with Cristal and smiled. She responded to him with a quick wave and turned her attention to the kids.

Darla and Dale, the twins, ran to greet their Uncle Malik with a big bear hug around his knees. Devona and Dahlia, the two older girls, settled for giving him a kiss on each cheek. Devona was 12 and Dahlia 11 so they thought they were getting a little too old for bear hugs. The twins were only five.

"So why is your Unk getting all the love?" Cristal pouted with one eye open. "Doesn't your Aunt Cristal deserve a little kissy-poo, too?"

"Sure!" They shouted in unison and attacked her until she fell backward onto the pink chiffon couch.

"That's enough of that roughhousing!" Chantilly scolded. "There'll be time for civilized play later when you children go upstairs to the romper room." She'd provided a fully stocked playroom for her grandchildren on the second level; everything from a bounce house to the very latest in video games. "Is that clear?" Chantilly added.

"Yes, Tia." The kids recited. Tia means Aunt in Spanish, and that's as close to Grandmother as Chantilly Moore was willing to go.

"Sis, your kids are growing up so fast." Cristal remarked.

"Yep; getting taller every time I see them." Malik beamed his perfect smile.

"And why is that so surprising?" Chantilly said coolly. That's what children do…when you have some."

Cristal shrank like a drooping blossom, and Malik draped his strong arm around his wife's shoulder for support.

"And what've you been up to, Malik?" Denver said, quickly changing the subject for Cristal's sake. "Business still booming for you, my man?"

"As long as these gang bangers keep killing each other off for no reason at all; you bet." Malik slid his eyes over to Chantilly. He couldn't figure the woman out. *Does she invite us over here for the sole purpose of sticking it to my wife?*

Chanel tried a little of the dip on a cracker. "Hmm," she said. "This is really tasty. You should try some, Cristal." She smiled slyly. "Manfred might be a keeper after all." Chanel's silky straight hair fell across her cute face, covering one trademark grey eye that she shared with her mother and sister. But unlike Cristal, she also shared her mother's light complexion. And although she'd managed to shed most of her baby weight, she was shorter than Cristal and she'd never have her knock-out figure.

"No, thanks." Cristal shook her head. "I've lost my appetite."

"What's wrong with you, now?" Chantilly sounded exasperated. "You shouldn't have come if you're in one of your moods."

"No mood, Mother." Cristal defended herself. "Just don't want no cracker."

"How many times must I tell you not to bring that hood-rat lingo into my home?" Chantilly snapped. "If you had agreed to go off to boarding school like Chanel, here, instead of talking your poor father into sending you to that horrid public high school—"

"How many times we gonna go over this, Mother?" Cristal snapped back. "I've been outta high school…what…over twelve years; and Daddy's been dead…what…more than five; so can we just drop it?"

"Yeah, Chantilly." Malik winked at Cristal. "I like the way my wife talks. I think it's kinda sexy."

41

"You would." Chantilly retorted. "Cristal had the opportunity to attend any college money could buy." She fluttered. "She could have gone to Brown, like Chanel, or Mercer, like me. But instead, she insisted on marrying straight out of high school."

"And I'm glad she did." Malik squeezed his wife's shoulders.

"Well, if you ask me, I think Chanel made the smarter choices." Chantilly swirled her eyes over to Denver, seeking to rally his support.

"Leave me out of this," Denver said in Cristal's defense. "I'm not the one to make the call."

"Well, thank God, Cristal was her father's favorite." Chantilly flamed. "Because the smartest thing he ever did was to talk you into marrying her, Malik…instead of one of those other no-accounts she dragged home."

Cristal rose up off the couch, and Malik tugged her back down. "Cristal was my choice," Malik said emphatically. "I'm thankful for Mr. Moore's friendship. He was my Big Brother, and he helped me get started in business." He stroked his wife's hand tenderly. "But nobody talked me into marrying Cristal. I met her at that 'horrid public high school'; remember?"

"So what did that clinic down in Houston have to say?" Chantilly eyed Cristal. "Are you going to be like your sister, here, and give me grandchildren? Hmm?"

"I—" Cristal shivered, and Malik squeezed her hand.

"When we have news," Malik said acidly, "we'll be sure to share it with you."

"And if I was my Father's favorite," Cristal's voice cracked like fragile glass, "it's only because Chanel, here, has always been yours."

"Not true!" Chantilly shot back. "Cristal, you've always been difficult. No reason for you to stop now—"

"Most definitely." Chanel raked Cristal with a snarly glance. "Forever the drama queen—"

"Is that dinner ever going to be ready?" Denver clapped his freckled hands to move Cristal out of the line of fire and to wipe that smug look of satisfaction off his wife's face. "The kids are starving," he added, "and they want to get up to that playroom. Right kids?"

"Eat! Eat! Eat!" The four carrot-topped children chanted, given their dad's opening.

"And I'm sure you agree, Mother." Chanel sniffed haughtily, while sending Cristal a chilling stare. "If Manfred is going to continue to serve us, he must realize your grandchildren have a need for speed." She giggled. "Get it?" And turned to Denver for confirmation, but his eyes bypassed her and rested on Cristal's sad countenance.

"Indeed!" Chantilly clucked. "We must certainly follow your children's wishes, since these may be the only grandchildren I'll ever have."

Malik's handsome features hardened into bronzed granite. Cristal's face crumbled like a broken doll.

At that very moment, Manfred entered the great room. "Madame," he announced grandly, "dinner is served."

CHAPTER 8
Jasmine

Jasmine re-checked the length of her new, black skirt as she pushed open the glass doors leading to the Fellowship Hall at First Morning Glory Church. She'd loved the skirt from the moment she tried it on at La Femme Boutique in the Galleria. She liked the way it flattered her shapely legs and flattened her bulging tummy, but she didn't want to cause a stir among the other women. She'd noticed the way some of them had treated a newcomer to Bible Study when she'd had the nerve to wear a red mini, over black fishnets. Poor woman never returned.

Although the fabulous stained-glass windows in the sanctuary and the thousands in attendance on Sunday mornings may have attracted Jasmine to First Morning Glory, it was the Women's Bible Study that had become near and dear to her heart. Of course, attendance at Bible Study was optional, Tuesdays at noon. But Jasmine had arranged her nursing schedule so she could make it nearly every session. She was thankful for the safe haven it offered from her fractured home life, and an opportunity to share with the 'sisters' she'd grown to love.

Even Dex had attended church with her sometimes when Madeline was home. His enviable good looks and easy manner had always created a stir in the pews on Sunday mornings. But, now, Madeline was gone. And like with so many other things in their relationship, she wasn't sure what would happen next. Her family was her life. But since Madeline's departure, everything seemed to be in a state of flux. She was walking a tight rope, gripping onto their fragile connections, and being with her sisters helped.

"Hello, Jasmine." Beatrice Garner greeted as she entered the Bible Study room. "It's about time you arrived."

Jasmine glanced at the prized, gold Rolex on her left wrist. It was the 25th wedding anniversary gift she'd received from Dex in June. "Am I late?" She scrambled for her place.

"Not really." Clara Clay said. "Beatrice just be pulling your chain, Girl."

"And you always let her." Marlana Gary giggled under her breath.

"Well, anyway." Jasmine fixed her smile. "Hello, my sisters. How is everyone?"

"We're fine." The other twelve women in the room chimed.

"If you'll take your seat, now, Jasmine." Beatrice glowered. "We can get started."

"Jasmine, how was your trip to D.C.?" Marlana whispered as Beatrice took to the podium.

"Fine." Jasmine's face creased. "Madeline got settled just fine."

"Then you're better than me." Clara's eyes crossed as she relived the memories. "I cried the whole way to Nashville and back when we dropped my son off at Fisk that first year." The serious injuries she'd sustained in a church bus accident some years back had left her with one good eye and one bad, and they had a tendency not to work together whenever she got upset or excited. But she was a feisty senior citizen with seasoned wisdom and a no-non-sense attitude. "I'm gonna fling off this thing as soon as I get home." She chortled as she yanked down on her salt and pepper wig with her thick, brown hands. "Don't even know why I wore this mess. Be itching me all over."

"And how is Dex?" Marlana smiled warmly. She was the youngest member of the group; an ex-college athlete, tall with twists. Her husband was in the ministry, and her children were still in grade school, except for her two youngest babies who she brought with her from time to time.

"He's fine." Jasmine lied. "We're fine—"

Clara traced the uncertainty in her eyes. "What is it, Jasmine?"

"Nothing." Jasmine's eyes clouded. "Everything is just fine."

"Ladies!" Beatrice cleared her throat to exert her authority. She was a gawky woman whose face looked as if it were at war with itself. Even when she attempted to smile, which was rare, her eyes and mouth seemed to be doing battle, with no apparent winner. She was probably never pretty, not even in her youth; but, at 45, she was a year younger than Jasmine, and she never let her forget it. Like Dex, her husband, Harold, was also a very successful defense attorney. But unlike Dex, her husband was well on his way to making partner at his firm, and she never let Jasmine forget that, either. At every National Bar Association event they attended in common, she flaunted her sense of superiority over the other lawyer's wives, particularly Jasmine.

"Ladies, if I can get your undivided attention." Beatrice insisted. "We will move on to our lesson for today."

Marlana covered her mouth with one hand. "Here we go, again," she whispered.

"Shush." Jasmine elbowed her playfully.

"If you will recall, ladies," Beatrice announced, "we agreed this quarter that we would study Ephesians 5 to get a better understanding of our role as wives."

"I've got an understanding." Someone chimed in from the back of the room.

"But we're after a Biblical understanding, my sisters." Beatrice clarified.

"We're all married women." A voice insisted.

"Yep, we've got husbands, whether we want 'em or not." Another woman chuckled.

"All the more reason we should learn what our Lord has to say about our station in life." Beatrice insisted. "We agreed, ladies," she said to stifle any further discussion.

Clara winked at Jasmine with her good eye. "I knew she'd take up all the oxygen in the room."

"Well, let's just get on with it." A voice blared from the back. "I'm hungry."

"In summary," Beatrice began, "Wives are to submit to their own husbands—"

"And husbands are to love their wives—" Another voice finished.

"Yeah-yeah." A lady snickered.

"Well, my Mom and Dad were soulmates for nearly 60 years." Beatrice sniffed proudly. "And my mother used to say, if the wife will do her part, the husband will follow suit. It is the wife who must at all times accept her role as nurturer, supporter and helper. If we do our part, our husbands will always play their part as breadwinners and caretakers of the home."

Clara raised her hand. "That's just your mother's opinion, Beatrice," she said, to the nods of the others. "Let's read the verses and see what the Lord has to say."

"Amen!" A chorus echoed.

"Then, indeed, let's get started." Beatrice propped her Bible onto the podium. "We were delayed by Sis. Jasmine because it's her turn to read." She signaled Jasmine for her to rise. "So please, come up here and begin reading at Ephesians, Chapter 5, Verse 22."

Marlana cleared her throat. "Excuse me," she whined. "Wouldn't it be better if we started at the first verse?" She turned to the others for support. "So we can read all the verses in context, I mean. It might give us a clearer meaning." Her confidence was teetering like a top. It usually didn't go well for people who stood up to Beatrice.

"Well, okay." Beatrice's mouth was saying, but her face was starting to do that crazy war dance again.

"And shouldn't we look up some other scriptures, so we can compare scripture to scripture to get a better understanding?" Clara piled on while Beatrice was gasping for air. "Ain't that what Pastor always tells us to do?"

"Who said that?" Beatrice scowled over the group until she caught a glimpse of Clara's crossed eyes hopping around in her head. "Oh, I should've known it would be you Clara Clay." She shot her a hot stare.

"But I think it is a good idea for us to study all the scriptures on the matter." Another voice floated from the back. "Because every husband and wife won't follow these instructions. And we need to know what to do then."

"That's right." Another voice chimed in. "We can only do our part."

"Well, all right, if it will move us along." Beatrice blustered. "Then Clara Clay, since this is your idea, you do the research—"

"Sure thing." Clara's good eye twinkled. "I'll get—"

"And, now, with no further ado." Beatrice's voice sliced right through the middle of Clara's thought. "Jasmine, start reading at Ephesians, Chapter 5, Verse 1. P-lease!"

CHAPTER 9
Leeza

"Dad! Coming in!" Leeza called out as she put her key in the lock to enter the two-story home where she'd grown up in Chestnut Hill, a northwest suburb of Philadelphia. She wanted to spare him the walk to the door. He'd sounded winded when she talked to him on the phone earlier that day.

Every time she crossed this stoop, she remembered her Mom kissing her there every morning before taking the commuter train into Center City. And sometimes, she wouldn't get back home from her magazine offices until nearly midnight. *If it hadn't been for Dad, I guess I would've been a latch-key kid like most of my friends.*

"How's my Sweet-Girl?" Her dad called out in his usual puffy greeting as he shuffled to meet her on his cane. His pale, white skin had a sickly pallor, and he was wearing his nasal cannula, which was connected by a tube to an air compressor to provide a steady flow of oxygen to his failing lungs. This tube was his lifeline, and it was long enough to allow him free access over the entire downstairs area. The home health nurse came in three times a week to make sure his face mask and other oxygen apparatuses were sanitized and fresh. When she was alive, he and his wife, Eliza, had slept upstairs in the master bedroom. But since his last bout with pneumonia, his whole universe consisted of the first floor of his home. He'd moved his bedroom downstairs, and he could no longer venture out pass the kitchen. The garage was off limits because it was too far and too damp. But it was just as well since he was no longer permitted to drive; nor could he tend to his beautiful flower gardens, or grow the vegetables he loved. He stayed in touch with friends on the telephone and the internet. He ordered his groceries and supplies online, and they were delivered to his front door. At age 56, Lee Manchester lived the true meaning of housebound.

"If you're fine, I'm fine." Leeza returned with her traditional greeting. They hugged each other tightly.

"Come on into the kitchen." Her dad beckoned. "I'm making your favorite dinner."

"Spaghetti and meat balls with garlic cheese toast?" Leeza sounded hopeful.

"You got it!" Her dad chirped.

"Nobody can make it like you, Dad." She praised. "Your angel hair pasta is always al dente, just like I like it."

"You've liked this dish since you were a little girl—"

"And you had to do all the cooking because 'your Mom was too busy being a Philadelphia big-shot.'" Leeza parroted his mantra; the one she'd heard all her life.

"You remember that, do you?"

"I remember you saying it, anyway," she said.

"Yes, those were some good ole days." Her dad recalled. "Just me and you in the kitchen after school—"

"After piano practice; after ballet practice; and—"

"Yeah, Kid," Lee said. "It was always just you and me."

"But that wasn't Mom's fault." Leeza quickly reminded him. "She was the breadwinner, and you were Mr. Mom." Leeza teased.

"I had no choice." Lee's voice tensed. "My ole ticker held me back." He clutched at his heart.

"I know, Dad. You don't have to explain it to me." She touched his shoulder. "I loved you being my very own, Mr. Mom."

"And you—" Lee wheezed. "You, Sweet-Girl, were my only reward."

"Smells good!" Leeza stirred the pot of bubbling marinara sauce. "That's what Mom would say every time she came home." She reminded him. "No matter what you were cooking, she always praised you."

"You're right. It's not your Mom's fault she soared to become Editor-in-Chief of Lifestyle INT, and I got sidelined with a bad heart." Lee's head drooped. "When my dream to be lead architect with Pi Corporation dried up, all I could land were a few drafting projects I could do from home."

"I know that wasn't your plan, Dad, but the three of us made the best of it, right?" Leeza smiled to lighten the mood. She'd been hearing his martyrdom routine—his twisted sob story—her entire life. All that was missing were the violins. "And you and Mom were a great team, remember?"

"Did you know that before your mother died in that plane crash five years ago, she'd taken that fashion magazine of hers from a nothing rag to an international success?" Lee shifted on his cane. "If it was happening anywhere in the world, it was happening in the glossy pages of Lifestyle INT."

"I know, Dad," Leeza said quietly, attempting to defuse his reverie.

Sensing he was losing his audience, her dad changed the subject. "But more importantly," he said, "how is my Sweet-Girl? How's your work going?"

Leeza perched on a bar stool and rested her elbows on the stone counter. "To tell the truth, Dad, it's getting pretty intense." She admitted.

"How so?" He frowned. "You know you can tell your ole dad all about it."

Leeza recounted her recent private conferences with her boss. "Mr. Cole is so fixated, Dad. He's dead serious about me landing three, new blue-chip clients in six months." Leeza whined. "This is the biggest challenge of my career."

"You can handle it." Her dad reassured her.

"But you don't understand, Dad. These are not run-of-the-mill clients on Mr. Cole's *secret* list. These are mega-billionaires from across the globe. They head up companies so vast you won't ever read about them in your local newspaper. And the heads of these enterprises are so wealthy, so elusive; they can fly under the radar." She rubbed her temples. "How will I ever be able to get close enough to three of them to pitch our services; to gain their confidence; to get their business—in six months?"

"You can do it, Sweet-Girl." Her dad wheezed with excitement. "Don't you see? This is our big break. This will put us over the top. This is what I've been grooming you for. This is your chance to strut your stuff!"

"Don't get so excited, Dad." Leeza cautioned. "We have a tough road ahead of us. Not only will this be a lot of gut-wrenching work over the next six months…but I also have a formidable opponent—"

"That Kyle Leary character?"

"Yes, Dad." Leeza smoothed her pageboy. "And he will fight me to the death to get his three, pick-of-the-litter clients before I get mine. He plays dirty, and he plays to win."

"That joker can't hold a candle to you, Leeza." Lee wiped his brow. "That's why I put you through the best schools money can buy. Me!" He pounded his chest so hard he coughed. "Remember?"

"Sure, Dad, I remember." Leeza reassured him. "And I appreciate your sacrifices—all of them. But Kyle can be ruthless—brutal. He's a good guy, but his hard-nosed tactics are legendary. That's why he's lasted at the company this long, without having the best education—"

"Well, don't you worry," her dad said, checking his pulse. "Class outstrips brass, every time. And the cream always rises to the top."

"Sure, Dad." Leeza moved into the dining room to set the table. "Dad, why do you still have these ratty, old placemats? Mom bought these before she…before the plane crash."

"You know me, Sweet-Girl," her dad said. "I'm a frugal man." He feigned a Scottish accent. "Can't throw a thing away, me Lassie." He gave her a wide grin. "And if I'm not careful, I'll become a horrible hoarder, and they'll be hauling me off to one of those ridiculous reality shows."

"Well, not to worry, Dad." Leeza teased. "I'll get you some new placemats for Christmas."

"Deal!" Her dad's smile sank into his rheumy eyes. "But in the meantime, let's eat!"

CHAPTER 10
Cristal

"What's up with this mood you're in Cristal?" Malik prowled around his living room like a big cat. It wasn't like him to come home for lunch, but he took the time to check on his wife. "You've been home from Houston, now, nearly a month, and all you do is mope around the house," he said.

"I know, Malik." Cristal purred and stretched out on the couch.

"This has to stop, Cris." Malik's voice showed signs of urgency. "You don't eat. You don't go out." He pointed to her outfit. "Look at you; slumming around in sweats, but you won't go to the gym. You're making yourself sick, and you're making me crazy."

"I'm trying." Cristal cuddled under her fuzzy, blue blanket.

"Is it the bad news you got at that clinic in Houston? Is that what's got you in this funk?" Malik's brow furrowed. "I know you had your heart set on them giving us some good news, Cris," he buzzed quietly. "I know you want a baby; I do, too."

"Yeah." She sighed. "Trying to deal with all that, too."

"So what else is it?" Malik propped himself against the grand piano. He wasn't moving until he got some answers.

"Malik…I just can't get over what Mother said—"

"When?" He blinked.

"When we were over there the other night."

"O-kay."

Cristal sat up and flung her feet to the floor. "I was just sitting there playing with Chanel's little, ginger-headed kids when Mother walked up to me—with her hair dyed to match—and says, 'Cristal, you must get your coloring from your daddy's side of the family because the rest of *our* family looks like me.'" Cristal's gray eyes flashed. "And she said it right in front of the kids, Malik! You didn't hear her?"

"You know your mom by now, Cris." Malik shook his head. "She barely has a kind word for anybody."

"She got plenty o' kind words for Chanel and her kids."

"So that's it, isn't it?" Malik paced back and forth. "You're still hung up on having a baby, just so you can please your mama."

"No, I'm not—"

"And you're jealous of your sister 'cause she's got some."

"No, I'm not!" Cristal blared. "I love Chanel and them kids, like they was my own, but my Mother doesn't have the right to throw it up in my face."

"I grant you the way Chantilly treats you is not cool." Malik slowed. "I don't like it, either, Babe. But whatcha gonna do? You can't change that woman!"

"Well, even if she don't love me; she oughta at least respect me." Cristal pouted.

"You can't make another human being respect you, Babe." Malik reasoned. "And what do you care? The Lord loves you. I love you. Haven't you been learning anything at church? Pastor Gabe is preaching on that all the time."

"I hear Pastor Gabe. I know what he says." Cristal twirled her wide eyes. "But it still hurts when my own Mother and Chanel try to dis' me."

"So you think having a baby will make your mom love you?"

"She might not love me, but she wouldn't be able to overlook me...and her grandchild."

Malik joined Cristal on the couch. He spread his hands on his muscular thighs and delivered his carefully chosen words. "Cristal, I love you. But it seems you won't be satisfied until your mother loves you, too."

"That's not true—"

"So, then, why're you sulking around here like a disappointed child?"

"Disappointed child?" Cristal eyes blazed, and she moved to the other end of the couch. "Is that how you see me?"

"Cris—"

"Malik, you don't know what I've been through!" she said, letting him have it. "You had to pee in a cup. But I'm the one who's been pulled on and shoved into; taken all kinds o' horrible shots, full o' who knows what…not you. All so I can have a baby…for us!"

"For us? Ha!" Malik scowled at her from his end of the couch. "That's not true, Cris."

"Not true?" She swirled her hands in dismay. "So why else have I been going through all this—"

"If having a baby was about *us*," Malik said, straining to hold his temper, "you'd be satisfied that I'm okay with it; however it goes."

"But—"

"But-nothing, Cristal! You want to have a baby just as much to compete with your sister as to please your mama." Malik hopped up. "And you treat me like I'm some kinda sperm donor."

"Not true!"

"It is true! If it weren't true you wouldn't be getting so upset about it." Malik's pent up frustrations had reached the boiling point. "You won't even let me touch you unless the moon and the stars are lined up just right for us to get pregnant. And all I ever hear is this-that-and-the-third about Chanel's kids, her family, and how your mother loves her grandkids. You're obsessed, Cris…and you're jealous."

"I am not jealous!" Cristal hopped up from the couch and stamped her barefoot on the plush carpet.

Malik's hand shot up to cut her off. "But while you're running around here worried about your precious family and what they think about you, let me give you a hot newsflash." He flung his words at her like well-aimed daggers. "Your sister is so self-absorbed; she could care less if you ever have a baby. And your dear-ole mom falls all over Chanel's kids for the simple satisfaction of poking you in yo eye." He jabbed with his finger. "And there is no way on God's green earth you're gonna ever please your mama. 'Cause for whatever reason, Cristal, that woman hates you. And your phony, asinine, kiss-up of a sister is her partner-in crime—"

"Watch yo'self, Malik!" Cristal growled.

"Cris, you care more about people who do nothing for you than you care about me." Malik boiled over. "You pay me no mind. You treat me cold. You ignore me." He spouted. "I even had to go to prayer meeting last night by myself. In fact, you haven't been to church with me since you got back from Houston." He seethed. "How do you think it makes me feel when everybody is praying and seeking the Lord for us to have a baby, and you ain't even there!"

"I'm tired of Pastor Gabe with all that ask-seek-knock mess." Cristal gave him as good as she got. "'Cause it ain't doing us no good!" She patted her firm, flat belly. "We ain't pregnant!"

"Jesus is Lord, Cris!" Malik took a deep breath and ramped down his anger. "That means He's in charge. He does things in His own way; in His own time."

"So if this Bible stuff ain't working, Malik, what's the point?" Cristal swirled her hands in the air.

"Jesus is not some genie in a bottle, Cristal Richardson." Malik gestured with his hands. "You can't rub Him three times and get three wishes."

"I know that." Cristal fumed. "But what's the point of praying over at that church, only to get disappointed over and over again?" Her eyes were burning with scalding tears. "I've gotta deal with this jacked-up mess…in my own way."

"Cris, we don't pray to make things happen." Malik's patience was being stretched like a rubber band. "We pray to let God know we love Him—"

"And then He'll bless us?" Cristal's brows rose expectantly.

"He blesses us all the time—"

"We ain't pregnant!"

"We breathing!" Malik sparked. "Just because the Lord doesn't do what we ask, when we ask, doesn't mean He's not blessing us." Malik strained. "He leads; we follow."

"But it ain't fair!" Cristal cried, unable to bear another word. "None of it's fair!"

"Maybe so." Malik came over and pinned her seizing body close to his firm chest. He hugged her hard and nuzzled her ear with his warm breath. "I know this hurts you, Babe," he said tenderly. "And it hurts me to see you hurt."

"Oh, Malik—"

"That's why I made us an appointment to meet with Pastor Gabe today."

"Pastor Gabe?" Cristal jerked back. "Without asking me—"

"Not up for discussion," Malik said, taking his rightful place. "Grab your jacket, Babe. He's waiting."

CHAPTER 11
Jasmine

The days stretched from September to November, and Jasmine felt the weight of them growing longer and lonelier without Madeline. When she was home, Jasmine could count on her daughter being there to greet her when she got home from work. But now, most days, she came home to an empty house. No Dex. No Madeline. The thick rubber soles of her work shoes squeaked against the custom hardwood floors. *There's nothing lonelier than a big empty house where a family used to live.* Unshed tears, which seemed to have taken up permanent residence, gathered behind her tired eyes.

Jasmine poured a steaming hot cup of coffee and settled in at the breakfast nook with a handful of sugar cookies. She was alone with her solitary thoughts. She found herself this way far too often. But she was holding onto the single shred of hope that things would get back to normal as soon as Madeline came home for Thanksgiving break.

It wasn't always like this. Jasmine's idle mind pushed replay, rewinding her life with Dex. *We were happy once. Weren't we?* She closed her eyes to dredge up memories of sweeter times when she first met the man who swept her off her feet. She poured another cup of coffee and let her mind scroll back to their first meeting. *My-my, I remember it like it was yesterday.*

***

"Hey, Pretty Lady." This very rich, very male voice was speaking over my head. I was just coming out of my biology lab in Greg Hall, so tired I flopped onto the steps with my load of books. I was terribly anxious about fall midterms the next day, so I was busily studying my notes when I heard this mellow voice say, "Girl, you'd better lighten up, or you're gonna blow a fuse."

When I finally looked up, I saw the most gorgeous man on campus. Sure I'd seen him before, every day since freshman year. Who could miss him? But in all our four years together at the University of Texas—the Mighty Class of 1988—he'd not said word one to me; nor me to him. I knew his name. Dexter Davis. Every female on campus knew his name during the day and dreamed about him every night. But I doubted seriously if he knew mine. So I squinted up into the sun and said, "My name's not Pretty Lady; it's Jasmine...Jasmine Mitchell.

"I know your name," Dex said with meaning and sat on the step next to me. "I'm Dex."

I sounded like J. J. of 'dyn-o-mite' fame when I said, "I know." And I hated myself as soon as the words slipped out.

Dex smiled at me, and the dimple in his right cheek lit up. In that moment, it felt like we were the only two people on planet earth. "I've admired you from afar," he said.

"Me?" I stuttered.

"Yes, you." Dex reiterated. "I like a woman who knows who she is and where she's going."

The way he said it put me at ease a little, and I said, "Well, I do know that. I've only had two dreams since I was ten—"

"And they are?" Dex's eyes probed me, like he was looking into my soul.

"I want to be a doctor...a pediatrician—"

"And the other?" His eyes softened into brown, round orbs that seemed meant only for me.

"To travel the world," I said, lowering my eyes to hide the longing he was planting deep inside me.

"I knew it." Dex nodded. "You've got your head on straight, and you know where you're going."

"I guess so."

"You remind me of my Mom." Dex confided. "Strong woman, my Mom. After Dad died, she fought for her dream, too."

I leaned into him as much to enjoy his aroma as to hear his words. "What was it?"

"She had always wanted to be a world-class chef, and she did everything in her power to make it happen."

"Is she a chef, now?" I was starting to feel like I'd known beautiful Dex Davis my whole life.

"Nope. She died before she could complete her training." His lids drooped. "But, I have no doubt, she would've made it. She was a wonderful, strong woman, my Mom."

"I'm sure she was, if you're any indication," I said, and to this day I don't know why.

"I know you are, too, Jazz," he said, using a nickname that no one else would've dared. "I told you; I've been watching you. You're going to make it. You've hardly looked up from your books these four years. You never come to any parties—"

"I'm pre-med," I said, a little defensively. "Lots to do."

"I'm pre-law; I know the feeling." Dex nodded. "But c'mon, every now and then we're expected to have some fun. They want us to be well-rounded, you know.

"That might be so." I straightened. "But *they* aren't pre-med."

Dex chuckled and the dimple in his right cheek seemed to shine just for me. It sent chills down to my core. *I can still feel them now.*

"Tell you what." Dex nudged me playfully. "We're seniors, now. We've come this far. So how 'bout me and you sharing a burger and fries…together? My treat."

My mind was racing. Dex Davis was asking to spend some time…with me! But I could barely breathe and my tongue weighed a ton like the pile of books in my lap. I was finally able to squeak out, "But I've got a major test tomorrow and—"

"And it'll take us all of 30 minutes." Dex urged. "And even pre-med majors have to eat."

As I was fishing around for a response, Dex was gathering up the load of books from my lap. His hand accidentally grazed my naked thigh, and my brain disengaged. Wham! Every nerve in me flooded to that one spot and sent me flying like a kite without a string. The sensation was terrible…and wonderful.

"Tell you what." Dex persisted. "I'll carry this boatload of books back to your dorm. And you can freshen up that pretty face of yours, and we'll share a meal."

"But don't you have a girlfriend?" I heard myself saying. "Beverly—"

"I've had lots of girlfriends," Dex said candidly. "But I'm looking for a wife."

I bobbled off the step, and Dex made sure his shoulder was at the ready to steady me. He towered over me—his 6'2" to my 5'4". But I'll admit it; I did look kinda hot that day with my hair flowing and my skirt short and cute. It was a warm day, and my shapely legs— my best asset—were smooth and bare. "But—"

"I'm not taking *no* for an answer." Dex smiled again and that blasted dimple flashed me like a strobe light.

My knees went weak. I was hooked. "Okay." I finally agreed, trying to sound like Dex Davis asked me out every day of the week. "But I've got to warn you," I said, "those books are heavy."

Dex juggled the load and slumped playfully. "Yes, I know." He scrolled over me with an accepting eye. "And I don't know how a cute, little thing like you can handle this load…alone." He led the way to my dorm. "But we'll see what we can do about that. And if my plan sticks, maybe we'll have a lawyer *and* a doctor in the family."

And that's how it all began. Me and Dex. We were inseparable from that day forward. We were soulmates. *But even then, I thought it was all just too good to be true.*

***

Jasmine poured herself another cup of coffee and settled in at the table. She was shaken out of her sweet reverie when Dex pushed open the door from the garage. "Dex?" she said, startled.

"Yeah, who were you expecting?" Dex said sourly. "Jack the Ripper?"

"No." Jasmine stoked some spark into her smile. "I'm glad it's you. I just didn't hear your car pull into the garage."

"I didn't. I left it in the driveway." He opened the refrigerator door and stood inside.

"I didn't know whether or not to expect you—"

"I see." Dex slammed the refrigerator door shut. "The one night I get home at a decent hour, and there's nothing here to eat."

"I can fix you something." Jasmine rose from her place at the table.

"Don't bother," Dex said caustically. "I have to go out later. I'll get something then."

"It's good to see you." Jasmine tried to lift her spirits. "What brings you home?"

"Yeah, well, a guy's got to get a change of clothes, sometimes." Dex propped onto the counter. "The Dunston trial...the one I've been working so hard to try to come up with a winning strategy...it goes to court in the morning. And I've got to look my best."

"Good." Jasmine offered. "Then let me make you a nice hot meal, draw you a nice hot bath, and—"

"Like I said," Dex interrupted, "don't bother. I just need my good pin-striped suit and a couple of white shirts...to go."

63

"Have you given any thought to what I might need, Dex?"

"Oops," he said dryly. "Here we go again, huh? You and your needs!" His voice rose with every syllable.

Jasmine left her hot coffee cup and followed him into the hallway. "I just want us to spend some time together—"

"Did you just hear anything I said to you, Jazz?" Dex looked at her like she was a failed biology experiment. "I am busy. I am in a fight for my client's very life. And all you can think about is us spending some time together?" He waved his hands overhead like he was losing it, while backing his way to the stairs. "This is choice...even coming from you, Jasmine. Choice!"

"Why do you do this, Dex? Why do you turn everything around...twist my words—"

"Have it your way, Jazz." Dex put his back to her and climbed the stairs to the second floor.

"What's happened to us, Dex?" She flashed back again to their beginnings. "We used to be so close."

"Nothing has happened, except your warped expectations." Dex turned on her at the top of the stairs. "We're not teenagers, Jazz. I don't have the luxury to cater to your every whim. I'm busy making a living. And if you haven't noticed, I'm trying to make partner at the firm. This could be my last chance."

"I get it, Dex." Jasmine pleaded from the bottom of the stairs. "I'm in full support of your career plans. That's not—"

"So why is it from where I stand, it sounds like a bunch of whining?" Dex blared. "You'd think you'd be supporting me every step of the way, instead of being so...needy." He shook his head woefully. "Don't you see it, Jazz? What's good for me is good for us—our family."

"Yes, I do. And I admire you for your ambitions. I truly do." Jasmine reasoned. "But do we have to pay for your success at the expense of our relationship—our marriage?"

"I see there's no use talking to you, Jasmine." Dex snapped. "You've got the worst case of tunnel vision I've ever seen. You can't see the big picture for straining at the nonessentials. What I'm doing now won't last forever. And when it's over, we'll all be the better for it—me, you and Madeline." He marched into their bedroom to pack his clothes for trial.

"Oh, Dex!" Jasmine gripped the handrail. "Why can't you hear me?" She crumbled onto the lush carpet on the bottom step.

After a few minutes, Dex stuck his head around the bedroom door. "By the way, Jazz," he said, "the partners are sponsoring a Fall Picnic for the firm and some of our best clients." He emerged with his packed leather bag and a matching garment bag. "It's supposed to be a big deal."

"When?" Jasmine braced up on the banister as Dex descended the stairs.

"Saturday in Fort Worth at the O.K. Corral," he said. "We want to get it done before Thanksgiving is upon us."

"Saturday?" Jasmine arched her back. "This Saturday?"

Dex cast a critical eye over his wife from her fuzzy slippers to the strands of wiry gray in her unruly 'fro. "Fix yourself up, Jazz." His words jabbed her like a pointed stick. "We're on the same team, Hon. And how you look is a reflection on me." He forced a smile. "And I want you to look good when you meet me at the picnic on Saturday."

"Meet you there?" Jasmine's face pinched. "But where'll you be—"

"I'll be at my office Friday night." Dex banged his bags onto the floor. "Most likely re-building my strategy for the Dunston case after the jury selection is finished on Friday."

"But why can't you come home?" Jasmine sputtered. "I was hoping we could go out to dinner on Friday night and spend some time—"

"That's not going to happen, Jazz." Dex shifted his weight to show his displeasure at having to repeat himself. "But I tell you what." He granted her a tight smile. "Since you are such an asset to my team, I'll swing by on Saturday and pick you up. How's that?" He said it like he was throwing a dog a bone. "Anyhow, it'll probably look better if we don't arrive in separate cars."

"But this is Tuesday, Dex. Are you saying I won't see you until Saturday?"

"The case, remember?" He squinted at her in disbelief. "I can't be bouncing back and forth across the Metroplex with the jury selection going on. I've gotta stay focused. Stay sharp. Pick the right jury. You should know by now how vital that is to my winning this case."

"Well, okay." Jasmine shrank into place.

"And, oh, Jazz." Dex towered over her and put his hands on both of her shoulders. "I need you to bring some of your *world-famous* brownies, too."

"Brownies?"

"Yes, wife-o'-mine." Dex schmoozed. "The brownies you brought to the summer picnic made a big hit." He picked up his bags again and made his way toward the exit. "I was talking to Susan Granger the other day—the partner's wife—"

"Yes, I know Susan." Jasmine trailed him into the kitchen.

"Of course, you do." Dex smiled. "Well, she came by to have lunch with Dave the other day, and she said the Fall Picnic would not be a hit without your *world-famous* brownies. I didn't think she'd remember." Dex smiled. "So prepare a big batch of them, Hon, and we'll wow the crowd." He worked his face into a silky grin. "I need all the brownie points I can get. Get it?"

"How long have you known about this picnic, Dex?" Jasmine's voice drooped.

"Oh, it's been on the calendar since the first of the year…but I wasn't even sure it was worth my time—"

"Until you talked to Susan Granger." Jasmine flopped back into her kitchen chair, feeling like a giant elephant had landed in the pit of her stomach.

"So will you do it, Hon?" Dex came and stood over her chair.

"Sure." Jasmine groaned, trying to put into practice the lessons Beatrice had drummed into their heads at Bible Study. "Reverence your husbands, ladies," Beatrice had shrilled in her familiar, grating voice. "Support your husbands in every way. This is our charge."

But try as she might to live up to Beatrice's *charge*, Jasmine couldn't prevent the sting of bile rising up in her throat, making her want to curse and scream and act like a crazy person. But as usual, she choked it back down; another dose of poison to her soul.

"See you Saturday," Dex said as he headed for his car, bags in tow. "And don't forget those *world-famous* brownies."

"Sure." The word dripped off Jasmine's lips like a leaky faucet as she gripped the handle of her cup. The coffee was as cold and stale as the kiss Dex planted in the middle of her forehead on his way out.

CHAPTER 12
Leeza

"Kyle!" Leeza ranted. "You didn't tell me you'd picked the only three American-based companies on Mr. Cole' secret list!"

"You didn't ask." Kyle stuffed his hands into his pockets.

"Do you think that's fair?" Leeza persisted. They were standing outside her office, and she was trying to tone it down even though she was furious.

"Cole came to me first, Leeza." Kyle gave as good as he got. "Why would I pick the companies that would make me a globetrotter when I could have my pick-of-the-litter right here in the States?"

"But that makes me have to circle the globe to meet my prospects." Leeza groaned.

"And that's my problem, how?" He gave her a wry smile.

"Kyle!" Leeza stamped her foot on the thick carpet in the hallway.

"All the better to beat you, my dear." Kyle blared. "I told you this was war. You don't think I'd leave the prime companies on the table, do you?"

"Oh, Kyle." Leeza relented. "This is going to be so hard."

"So which ones did you pick?" Kyle shrugged.

"I—" Leeza stopped herself. "I guess I shouldn't tell you, huh, since we're at war?"

"Suit yourself." Kyle smirked and pushed open her office door. "But I do have some news I can share about Brandi-the-Slut," he whispered.

"What?" Leeza followed Kyle into her office and flipped on the light.

"Brandi was caught snooping around Mr. Cole's office while his secretary was at lunch." Kyle buzzed.

"And what was her excuse for being in our boss' office?" Leeza tensed.

"Said she was looking for Cole's secretary." Kyle made it a point to close the door. "But pretty much nobody believes her 'cause her boss, Dan Skinner, will have absolutely no dealings with Cole until after the promotion is announced in March—"

"March!" Leeza sweated. "Don't remind me. We've only got six months to get these new super-clients for Cole, and the clock is ticking."

"Tick-tock." Kyle rocked back on his heels for emphasis. "But it's a good thing Mr. Cole had his secret file under lock and key, or our pretty, little Brandi might have swiped it."

"Guess it's not enough she's sleeping with one of the partners?"

"Nope. Don't know if she was after it for herself or for Skinner, but she's capable of anything to get her boss promoted—"

"And herself promoted!"

"And she's gone too far to turn back now."

Leeza narrowed her eyes. "She is a sneaky, little bird."

"But all is fair in love and war." Kyle taunted her with a wicked wink. "Speaking of which, Leeza, I think I might have my first new client in the bag."

"I would guess so." Leeza blustered, although it was news she'd dreaded. "You have the decided advantage."

"Nothing definite, mind you." Kyle growled like a tiger. "But I am on the prowl. Got my big guns trained on my first U.S. company, and I've got 'em in my sights."

"Kyle, you're awful." Leeza backed out of her office, leaving him there to gloat. "Turn out the light." She pouted. "I've got a plane to catch."

CHAPTER 13
Cristal

Malik and Cristal sat in silence during the hour long drive to New Bethel Church to meet with Pastor Gabrielle Lassiter. She was still smarting over the tongue lashing he'd given her at home. He'd administered his words with keen precision, and they'd cut her like a knife. He'd even made this appointment with Pastor Gabe behind her back. But didn't Malik understand that not being able to have a baby was killing her already? Did he have to stick it to her, too?

Cristal stared at nothing through the passenger side window. Malik's knuckles were tight on the steering wheel as he moved his sleek, black Mercedes through the dense Atlanta lunch time traffic on I-85 North. Malik had grown up in New Bethel. His mother, Sis. Lois, had brought him to Sunday School and church every Sunday. Malik would complain when she tried to drag him to evening services, and his daddy often rescued him from the prospect. But Pastor Gabe was family. He'd buried Malik's mother, and he'd taken his dad's place over the past fifteen years since his death. And since Cristal's family had no church home to speak of, he and Cristal were married there, too.

Pastor Gabe was waiting for them in his church office when they arrived. The memorabilia on his wall attested to his interests in cycling, fishing and other outdoor pursuits. His enthusiasm for communing with nature was legendary, and his lean body and sharp mind were proof of its benefits. He was a statesman like Mandela; a praying man like Dr. King. His graying afro and wiry beard could be off-putting, but his compassionate tone and tolerant manner endeared him to his congregation. When asked why he was not more forceful in his preaching style and more heavy-handed in his dealings like some of his fellow mega-church pastors, Pastor Gabe was quoted as saying, "I love the God of the Bible, and I believe His word is well able to do the work. He doesn't need me jamming it down His people's throats."

Pastor Gabe greeted them warmly when they arrived. "Come in. Take a seat," he said. Cristal and Malik occupied the chairs set out in front of his desk, which was deeply mired in stacks of books and papers. Cristal scooted her chair away from Malik. He scooted his chair closer to hers. She gave him a look.

Pleasantries aside, Pastor Gabe launched right in. He'd known Malik and Cristal too long for idle chit-chat. "Malik tells me you got some so-so news from that fertility clinic down in Houston." Pastor Gabe motioned toward Malik who was sitting to his right.

"Not so-so." Cristal swirled her eyes in Malik's direction. She was leaning as far away from him as she could. "No-go." She pouted. "They said my womb couldn't hold a baby even if they implanted one of our own embryos."

"Medical science can do some unimaginable things these days—"

"But they can't do this." Cristal pouted. "Me having a baby would take a miracle."

"Well, isn't that what we've been praying for, Cristal?" Pastor Gabe propped his hands behind his head. "Me and all the ministries have been coming together to pray for a miracle for you and Malik."

"I know, Pastor Gabe." Cristal granted. "And I'm grateful. It's just that—"

"You can't give up hope, Cristal." Pastor Gabe insisted. "You and Malik have to keep the faith."

"I've been keeping it." Cristal shook off Malik's attempt to hold her hand. "But we ain't pregnant."

Pastor Gabe straightened in his chair. "When Malik told me about this latest news, a couple of scriptures came to mind—"

"It ain't the latest news, Pastor." Cristal bristled. "It's the last news."

"I understand what you're saying, Sis. Cristal." Pastor Gabe stiffened his resolve. "But are you interested in hearing my scriptures?"

"Okay. Sure, Pastor. I'll listen to your scriptures." Cristal swirled her eyes over at Malik. "That's why we're here, ain't it?"

Not wanting to lose his audience, Pastor Gabe jumped right in. "So here's the first one," he said. "Romans 1:17 tells us, 'The just shall live by faith.'" Pastor Gabe smiled.

"I know that." Cristal glowered.

"We're saved when we trust Jesus," Pastor Gabe continued. "Now, we must live by trusting Jesus. We must live everyday believing He's already done whatever we need."

"O-kay." Cristal rocked her neck.

Pastor Gabe excused her impertinence for pain. "He wants us to trust His plan for our lives."

"I do trust Jesus." Cristal crossed her eyes like Pastor Gabe was losing it. "I got saved in this very church. That's why I been praying—"

"But you're praying for what you want, Cris." Malik couldn't resist jumping in. "Not for God's will to be done."

"How am I s'posed to know what His will is? All I know is what I want." She spouted. "I thought it was what we both wanted, Malik."

"Babe." Malik grabbed her hand in spite of her resistance. He laced his fingers through hers. "You know I want you to have our baby." The truth of his words rang so true; a lump rose in Cristal's throat.

"Well, does anybody want to hear what the Bible has to say?" Pastor Gabe's patience was waning. "That's what's wrong with the world today," he said prophetically. "Nobody wants to hear what God has to say about anything."

"Sure, Pastor. Please, go on." Malik coaxed.

72

Pastor Gabe shook off his annoyance and continued. "Hebrews 4:10 says, 'For he that is entered into His rest, he also hath ceased from his own works, as God did from his.'"

"Huh?" Cristal shook her head.

"When we accept Jesus, He wants us to rest from our own works." Pastor Gabe summed up. "He has already put in place everything that's going to happen, and we have to trust Him and accept that His will in every matter is right and good." Pastor Gabe smiled. "Even if we don't like it or understand it."

"That's right, Pastor." Malik tossed in his amen.

Cristal's face turned stony and her body knotted up. She felt so alone.

"Don't you see, Cristal." Pastor Gabe pleaded. "The Lord wants us to cease from all of *our* works…and rest in all of *His* works…like He did on the seventh day."

"I don't get it." Cristal breathed.

"In other words," Pastor Gabe said patiently, "Jesus wants us to stop trying to force what we want and rest in what He's already prepared for our lives. Otherwise, we'll be in constant turmoil if we keep trying to impose our will over His."

"So what you saying?" Cristal's voice cracked in frustration. "The Lord don't want me to try to have a baby? That I should just sit back and do nothing?"

"Of course, not," Pastor Gabe said quietly, trying to offer her some solace. "The Lord wants you to try. He wants you and Malik to *get it on*." He grinned broadly. "Believe me; I ain't so old I don't know about these things. But the Lord also wants you to leave the outcome to Him."

"That's right." Malik agreed.

"And if you want this baby to please Him, and for no other reason," Pastor Gabe said, "you'll be able to rest in whatever He allows."

"But didn't you say to pray for what I want?" Cristal rolled her neck.

"Yes, I did, Cristal." The pastor nodded. "But sometimes we don't know our own hearts. We can have mixed motives that only the Lord knows."

"That's right." Malik flapped.

Pastor Gabe smiled at both of them consolingly. "We can think we're ever so clear on what we want and why. When in actuality, it can be for other reasons entirely."

Malik couldn't help closing in. "What he's saying, Cris, is if you're trying to have a baby to please your mama that may not be the Lord's will for our lives."

"Say what?" Cristal nearly jumped out of her chair.

"Hold on, Malik." Pastor Gabe raised his hand to prevent a blood bath. "All I'm saying is we don't even have to worry about our motives if we trust the Lord to give us what He wants us to have."

"We pay our tithes, Pastor!" Cristal took a different tact. "Are you saying we ain't gonna be blessed?"

"We are blessed." Malik seethed. "We're here; we're alive; we're healthy; we've got each other—"

"Don't get stupid, Malik!" Cristal swirled her eyes on him. "You know what I mean. I want a baby. We want a baby."

"We're praying." Pastor Gabe broke in before things got worse. "We've laid your petition before the Lord. Now, the timing and the outcome is in the Lord's hands; not ours."

"We have to deal with what is, Babe." Malik pleaded. "Not with what we want it to be—"

"That's easy for y'all to say." Cristal was close to tears. She felt as if the whole universe was ganging up on her. "Y'all don't have to watch the clock ticking by every month and see yourself no closer to having a baby than you were the month before—"

"Keep the faith, Sis. Cristal—"

"Stop it!" Cristal cried. "We keep going 'round in this same circle, Pastor. How am I s'pose to hold onto my faith when y'all keep telling me the Lord ain't gonna answer my prayer?"

"He's just saying we can't make it happen, Cris." Malik tried to calm her. "Babe, we've gotta accept the Lord's will...whatever it is—"

"Y'all be trippin'!" Cristal jumped up. "No disrespect, Pastor Gabe. I appreciate everything you've done, but this dream-bashin' session is over!"

"But Cristal—" Pastor Gabe pleaded.

"Y'all acting like a bunch o' haters up in here, and I'm outta here!" Cristal stormed to the door. "You coming, Malik?"

CHAPTER 14
Jasmine

"I had a good time." Dex pecked Jasmine on the forehead as they entered their house through the garage entrance. "What about you, Jazz?"

"Yes, thank you, Dex." Jasmine eked out a smile. "The Partner's Fall Picnic was something special all right. I bet your clients were really impressed."

"That was the idea," Dex said. "We roll out the red carpet and pull out all the stops for the clients who pay the bills."

"Want some coffee?" Jasmine offered as they settled into the kitchen.

"Sure." Dex sat at the counter. "I'll take a cup of your *world-famous* coffee," he said with a grin, "if it's half as good as your *world-famous* brownies."

"Okay." Jasmine set to programming the coffee maker. She changed it to four cups, rather than her normal two. Her heart was humming, happy that things seemed to be getting better between her and Dex. "I had a nice chat with Susan Granger," she said.

"I'm glad you did." Dex smiled. "If I'm going to make partner, I need all of the wives to love you." He looked at his wife admiringly. "And what's not to love."

Jasmine was at her best. She'd spent some quality time at the salon and the nail shop for the occasion. She'd even found some western wear that slimed her hips and didn't make her look so pudgy. "They're an easy bunch to get along with." Jasmine smiled. "The wives are pretty down to earth and not catty like some of the ladies at my church."

"Do tell." Dex's dimple glimmered at her.

Jasmine set a coffee mug before him and took a seat on the stool across from him. It felt good to have her husband home. "You want cream or sugar?" she asked.

"No, this is fine." Dex smiled.

"So, how's the trial coming?" Jasmine savored the hot brew.

"Fine. Better than I'd expected, actually." Dex took a sip. "I think the jury will be alright."

"Good," Jasmine said easily. "I'm glad." She reached across the counter to touch his hand, but Dex moved it away and gripped his mug instead.

"Talked to my Baby-Girl today." He sipped.

"You did?" Jasmine took the hint and eased her hand back into its place. "I talked to her yesterday."

"Well, she called me when I was out on the golf course with my clients."

"What did she say?" Jasmine looked hopeful.

"Seems like she and her roommate have made fast friends." Dex chuckled.

"Not like you and…Reginald. Remember?" Jasmine giggled. "It was all over campus. You and your freshman roommate had to be separated a number of times to keep you from killing each other."

"Remember that, do you?" Dex smirked at the thought. "Well, it's not like that with Madeline and Imani; that's for sure."

"I know. She told me." Jasmine smiled. "Imani's dad is an Ambassador to the United Nations and a high-ranking official in the Nigerian government."

"Yes, I know." Dex grinned. "That's what I'm paying for; it's one of the advantages of a good education at a prestigious college. Madi can cultivate a great network of friends and allies that will serve her for a lifetime."

"Yes." Jasmine got up to freshen her cup. "That is great."

"Madi called to ask my permission," Dex said while her back was turned.

"Oh?" Jasmine returned to her place at the counter.

"She asked me if she could spend the Thanksgiving break with Imani and her family." Dex risked a glance at Jasmine.

"What?" Jasmine flared. "I just talked to her yesterday, and she didn't say a word—"

"She called me, Jazz." Dex blared. "She asked my permission."

"And what did you say?" Jasmine tensed.

"Of course, I said, yes." Dex put his hands palm down on the counter. "What a super opportunity—"

"Without discussing it with me?" Jasmine shrilled.

"Discuss it with you?" Dex snapped. "I don't have to discuss it with you. I'm her father. She asked my permission. And I gave it to her. End of story."

Jasmine was feeling lightheaded. She gripped the counter to prevent herself from taking a tumble off the stool. "But I was looking forward to us being together again…as a family—"

"But you see, that wasn't going to happen anyway," Dex said coolly. "That's why I decided it was just as well that Madeline spend the time getting to know Ambassador Acho and his family—"

"Why?" Jasmine said dizzily. "Why was it not going to happen anyway?"

"Because I'm not going to be here, either." Dex slammed his hand on the top of the counter.

"What?" Jasmine sputtered, nearly falling backward.

"I'm playing golf in Ft. Lauderdale over the Thanksgiving holiday."

"Golf? Florida?"

"Yes. Florida." Dex's voice spiked like he was talking to a dumb-witted child. "One of my clients invited me to spend the holidays at his beachfront home down there."

"But what about me?" Jasmine said more to herself than to her idiot husband; and just when she thought things might be improving between them.

"What about you, Jazz?" Dex said smartly, hostility glowing in his face. "Seems to me like you need to start making plans of your own and stop trying to pull us into them." He shot up from the counter. "Madeline is finally on her own—out from under your selfish control. And I'm busy forming the kind of business connections I need to get a shot at making partner before I'm too old to care. Get it?"

Jasmine was afraid to move. Her heart was pounding so fast she thought she might pass out. She held onto her cup—speechless.

"And don't give Madi a hard time about this either." Dex warned. "It's my decision to make. And I made it." He slammed the door to the garage on his way out. "I'm going back to the office."

CHAPTER 15
Leeza

Leeza broke into Mr. Cole's office in a full trot, without the benefit of an appointment. "I only need a minute of your time, Mr. Cole." She explained as she met his puzzled stare. His frazzled secretary was hot on her heels.

Dick Cole waved off his secretary, and she retreated to the outer office. "Sit down, Miss Manchester," Mr. Cole said. "And this had better be good."

"I have some exciting news, sir, and it just won't wait." Leeza entreated.

"Then take a seat." Mr. Cole turned to look at the clock on his credenza. It was barely Thanksgiving, but someone in the holiday spirit had snuck a miniature, lighted Christmas tree there, as well. "I can give you seven minutes," he said.

"You know the conglomerate in Argentina, Buena Vista?" Leeza said as she took her seat and crossed her legs.

"Yes, of course!" Mr. Cole exclaimed. "They're tops on my secret list."

"Well, score a point for our side!" Leeza cheered. "I got them to sign with us at dinner last night."

"You were in Buenos Aires last night?"

"Yes!" Leeza exclaimed. "I came straight here from the airport."

"Well, I'm indeed proud of you, Miss Manchester." Cole took a swig of his coffee. "You're making quite a reputation for yourself. But I'm interested to know; what tipped the scales in our favor? I know they were being courted by the likes of Black & Brewster, and they've been in the business over 50 years."

"That's just it, Mr. Cole," Leeza said excitedly. "Buena Vista was in the market for a fresh new face, a new approach to reach the youth market…and Señor Gremaldi said he liked mine." Leeza quickly clarified. "He liked my pitch, my presentation, my passion. He said my in-depth understanding of the younger generation would open up a whole new revenue stream for their new product lines."

"Well, I'm proud of your persistence, Miss Manchester. It gets me that much closer to my goal. If my team can bring in new, blue-chip business, I'll be a shoe-in for partner…I don't care what smoke and mirrors that devil Skinner has up his sleeves." Cole's chest swelled. "Besides, it seems Skinner dropped the ball on the Henderson deal, and I'm having to clean up his mess."

"Well, I guess my seven minutes are up." Leeza rose to leave. "But I just had to share the good news. I'm well on my way to getting the three new clients I need to follow in your footsteps once you've been promoted to partner." She pitched her ambitions.

"Well…about that, Miss Manchester."

"Yes—" Leeza's shaky hand smoothed her blonde pageboy.

"It seems that Kyle may get to the finish line before you—"

"What?" Leeza frowned. "Kyle has one new client, and now I have one—"

"That's where you're wrong, Miss Manchester." Cole slowed, not wanting to dampen Leeza's enthusiasm, or risk missing out on any new clients she could muster. "Kyle has managed to snag two, new blue-chippers to date."

"Two?" Leeza huffed. "So now it's two to one?" She flustered. "But…but it isn't fair, you know. It's so much easier for him, Mr. Cole. I'm the one with the handicap. Kyle has all of the North American prospects on his list, and I—"

"Now-now, Leeza, no sour grapes." Cole lowered his stained coffee mug to his desk. "We must be happy for each other when we have successes because it brings each of us that much closer to our desired goals."

"But I'm having to fly all over the world—"

"Sorry, Miss Manchester." Cole cut her short before the tears flooding her eyes could begin to flow. "Your time is up. My last appointment is waiting." He rose to show her the door. "Best of luck to you, Leeza, and please keep me posted on your progress. Happy Holidays!"

Leeza stumbled badly as she fled Mr. Cole's office and the convicting eye of his secretary. But she was glad she'd gotten in a big supply of watercolors. It would probably take her all night to paint away her frustrations.

CHAPTER 16
Cristal

Cristal opened the sunroof on her red Cadillac STS for the long drive to her mother's palatial home in Buckhead. Thanksgiving Day was unseasonably warm and she hated the idea of her mother being cooped up suffering with a terrible cold on such a glorious day. Chantilly had regrettably canceled the family's Thanksgiving dinner because she wasn't feeling well enough to go on with it, but Cristal decided to drop off the deluxe gourmet fruit basket she'd ordered for the occasion. Regardless of their differences, Chantilly was still family.

Mother really sounded pitiful over the phone. Cristal looked over at the bow-clad basket that was taking up the entire passenger seat. It was so big, in fact, she had to strap it in like a passenger. *Since I already ordered this big ole thang, I'll just drop it off and go. Maybe, it'll cheer her up.*

As Cristal drove up the long, white-stoned driveway, she slowed with a puzzled look on her face. Manfred's Catering van was parked in front of the four-car garage. And Chanel's family van was parked in the circular drive.

"What the—?" *Skreech!* Cristal pounded her brakes and sat there looking stunned for a moment. Then she eased open her car door, and without closing it behind her, she hustled over to the kitchen window on tiptoes; which was a feat in itself, sporting her five-inch heels. Sure enough, there they were—all there together—her mother, her sister, her sister's husband, and their kids. She saw it with her own eyes. Stumbling back to her car, Cristal crept out of the driveway and back onto the main road. On the freeway, the other traffic was a blur through her tears. Cristal didn't slow until she whirled into her own driveway on two wheels.

"Malik!" she yelled, hauling in the towering fruit basket. "You're not gonna believe this!"

"What is it?" Malik hustled to the door with a hot dog in one hand, slathered in mustard, onions, relish and chili, and a wad of paper towels in the other. He stowed his towels under his armpit and helped Cristal settle the huge fruit basket onto the floor.

Cristal sniffed. "You're not gonna believe this—"

"What?" Malik repeated. "Calm down, Cris, and talk to me."

Cristal sucked in a deep breath and crumbled onto the couch. "Mother lied!"

Malik wiped his mouth with one of the towels. "And what else is new," he muttered.

"I wouldn't have believed it, if I hadn't seen it with my own eyes." Cristal pursed her lips. "They're all over there, having Thanksgiving dinner…together!"

"Who?" Malik took another bite of his hot dog. "Calm down, Woman, and tell me what you're talking about."

Cristal folded her arms across her shapely cleavage to settle her pounding heart. "I drove up there to take Mother that big-A fruit basket over there—"

"Uh-huh."

"And Manfred's Catering truck was parked in the driveway." Cristal stormed.

"Uh-huh."

"So I gets out, all quiet like, and tiptoe to the kitchen window, right?" Cristal mimicked her steps. "And guess what I saw?"

"What?"

"Mother was having the family's Thanksgiving dinner with Chanel, Denver, and all their kids—without us!"

"O-kay."

"But she called me and cancelled Thanksgiving dinner because she said she was too sick to go on." Cristal explained.

"That's what she told you?"

"Yes, the lying heifer!" Cristal blared. "That's what she told me. But, actually, she was planning the family dinner without me, without us, all along!"

"O-kay."

"Okay!" Cristal screeched. "Is that all you can say?" She flailed her arms in Malik's face. "That woman lied to me—to us. They're having the family's Thanksgiving dinner without us…and that's all you can say?"

"You can just cool your jets with me, Cris," Malik said without flinching. "This is Thanksgiving Day, and you and your clan are not gonna mess it up for me…not any more than you already have."

Cristal took a step back and watched him take the last bite of his hotdog. "Whatcha mean…not any more than we already have?" she said.

"Evidently, your mother did not want to have Thanksgiving dinner with you—us—because she called you and cancelled it, right?" Malik said evenly.

"Right…but she lied!"

"She didn't lie to you," Malik said pointedly. "She cancelled with you because she didn't want you to be there. Can't you get that through your head, Cristal?"

"But we're family!" Cristal insisted.

"Oh?" Malik jabbed. "Are we?"

"Well, we're supposed to be." Cristal flared. "And she's got my stank sister and her husband and all their kids over there, but not us!"

"So, how long have you known that your mother had dis-invited you to her dinner party?" Malik quizzed.

"She called me Monday." Cristal frowned. "Saying she was too sick to carry on."

"And today is Thursday." Malik propped his muscular frame against the nearest wall.

"Yes, Thursday—Thanksgiving Day." Cristal smirked. "All day long."

"And me." Malik pointed to himself. "I'm here fending for myself, eating a hotdog for Thanksgiving dinner, while you're off taking that big-A fruit basket to your mother who didn't wanna see you anyway!" Malik's voice escalated with each syllable.

"But Malik—"

"But-Malik, nothing!" He swelled. "You had time to order a million-dollar fruit basket for your mother, to impress her and your uppity sister, but you didn't even take the time to order, let alone cook, a turkey and trimmings for your own family—me—us!" He wiped the crumbs off his hands onto a paper towel. "While you're out, way across town, I'm left here to fend for myself. And the best I can come up with in our house on Thanksgiving Day is a hotdog!"

Cristal covered the distance between them in an instant and wrapped her arms around his waist. "Oh, Malik." She cried. "I'm so sorry. I never thought—"

"That's just it." Malik peeled her off him and straight-armed her away. "You never think, Cris—not about me; not about me and you; not about our family. You only have room in your heart to think about your mother, and your silly sister, and her kids. That's who you consider your family."

"I do care about our family, Malik!" Cristal cried. "Why do you think I've been trying so hard to have a baby?"

Malik laughed, without an ounce of mirth. "And you know the funny thing about it?" He quickly answered his own question. "I love you, Cris, and you pay me no mind. You talk to me like I'm stupid; like I've got a tail. But your mother, who could care less for you, you love her to the moon and back." He walked back into the kitchen. "I guess I could get more outta you if I treated you like dirt, too, huh? Go figure!"

Cristal trailed behind him. "But Malik." She pled. "I'm sorry. You're right. I should have made sure we had our own Thanksgiving dinner when I realized we weren't invited to Mother's."

"So where was your head, Cris?" Malik turned and gave her a long, solemn look. "Where was your heart?"

Cristal stiffened under his gaze. "I said I'm sorry, didn't I?"

Malik snatched a knife out of the block on the counter, and Cristal backed away to give him some room. She'd never seen him so worked up. He marched into the living room, swung the knife at the big-A fruit basket and ripped the exquisite wrappings. He stabbed one of the exotic-looking brown pears with his knife and tore a bite out of it—unwashed.

CHAPTER 17
Jasmine

Beatrice Garner stood at the podium in front of the Bible Study Class and took a deep breath. "I trust each of you and your families had a delightful Thanksgiving season," she said gaily. "I know Harold and I did. We're starting to enjoy our empty nest since Harold, Jr. has been away at college." She breathed just long enough to continue. "Yes, we had a splendid time, just the two of us, husband and wife; just like the Bible tells us to." A few low groans rumbled in the back of the room. Everybody was sick of Beatrice and her incessant personal references, but nobody had the heart to tell her they were highly inappropriate.

"Well, it seems this week." Beatrice droned on, taking full privilege of her role as leader. "This is the week that Clara Clay is to discuss some other Bible verses pertaining to marriage. I have not been allowed to review her work in advance." Beatrice glared at Clara pointedly. She had demanded that Clara come over to her house to review her findings during the holidays, but Clara had graciously declined. "So I'm hearing this from Clara for the first time like the rest of you." Faint applause began to speckle the room trying to move the process along. "So I guess you're ready." Beatrice's face beat the war drums. "So come on up here, Clara and take my place at the podium; and let us hear what you have to say." Beatrice gave Clara another glaring look as she assumed her seat of honor on the front row. *That Clara Clay can never outdo me…her and her cross-eyed self.*

Clara was all smiles as she came forward. "Praise the Lord, everybody!" She rang out and everyone joined in. "Praise the Lord!"

"Now, my sisters, you know I'm not much of a talker." Clara smiled warmly. "Nothing like Beatrice, here." A few snickers emerged. "But I'll do my best." She added. "All the marriage scriptures I've looked up are included in your handout. Did everybody get one?"

Everyone nodded and held up their copy of the one-pager.

"Good," Clara said. "But there're only three scriptures I want us to focus on today."

"All right." Her short-and-sweet style gathered some encouraging nods.

Clara settled herself at the podium. "Now, I've heard a number of you ladies refer to your husbands as your 'soulmates'." She smiled. "But I can't find that term in the Bible, not one time."

She got some puzzled looks.

"Nope." Clara clarified. "Concerning our souls, Jesus has this to say: "Thou shall love the Lord thy God with all thy heart, and with all thy soul, and with all thy mind." (Matthew 22:37) "See it? It's there in your handout."

Everyone nodded in agreement as they checked it out.

"So if we're to love the Lord with *all* our soul, there ain't no room for our husbands in our souls." Clara firmed her hands on the podium. "Looks to me like the Lord is our only soulmate."

Some of the women looked relieved, like the final piece of a giant puzzle had been locked into place; others were frowning in disbelief.

"Now, before you tar and feather me right here where I stand." Clara teased. "The Bible does say we are to be 'one flesh' with our husbands. You'll find that reference in your handout, too." (Matthew 19:5)

"And that means sex." A voice snuck in from the back of the room. "For some o' y'all that ain't had none lately." Raucous laughter replaced the mounting tension.

"That's right." Clara agreed, happy for the help. "The Bible says we are to be one flesh with our husbands, and we're not supposed to withhold it from 'em either, y'all."

"Sure does." One of the ladies noted. "Look at this verse, right here." She pointed out. (1 Corinthians 7:5)

Clara cleared her throat and regained their attention. "So the Bible tells us our souls belong to the Lord, and our bodies belong to our husbands."

"Can't disagree with you there." Marlana giggled. "Because a soul is a mighty fragile thing to entrust into a man's clumsy hands."

"You're right, Sis. Marlana." Clara agreed. "Don't put nobody in your soul; that's too much responsibility for any human being to handle."

By this time, Beatrice's face was doing a war dance. Her mouth and eyes were fighting the good fight, and the winner was as yet undetermined.

"Turn in your Bibles to 1 Peter 3, 5-6." Clara invited. "I wanna show you something. We're almost done." Pages were flipping like a strong breeze had hit the room. "Sis. Jasmine will you read it for us?"

Jasmine did as she was asked. "'For after this manner in the old time the holy women also, who trusted in God, adorned themselves, being in subjection unto their own husbands. Even as Sara obeyed Abraham, calling him lord: whose daughters ye are, as long as ye do well and are not afraid with any amazement.'"

"Thank you, sister," Clara said. "So you see, ladies, it says here we are to be like Sarah, who trusted in God...but called her husband lord."

"And that's *little* lord." One of the ladies pointed out. "Not *big* Lord."

"In other words," Marlana said, picking up one of her babies, "Sara respected her husband, but she didn't put her trust in that lying joker."

"How dare you speak that way about Father Abraham!" Beatrice bristled. He was God's chosen—"

"And he was a man—"

"And he did lie!" Another sister interjected. "He nearly got Sarah raped by telling that king she was his sister—"

"When all he was trying to do was save his own sorry neck—"

"That's right. He sure did."

Clara reeled them back in. "But Sarah...*trusted* in God. That's the point." She reminded them. "Sarah honored and respected her husband, but Abraham was still her *little* lord—"

"And God was her *big* Lord."

"You got that right."

Clara laid her one good eye on Jasmine and said, "That means we don't have to belittle ourselves to hold onto our marriages." And then she crossed her eyes at Beatrice and said, "And it also means, we don't have to lie 'bout 'em, neither."

"That's right," Marlana said. She was jostling one of her restless babies on her knee. "Because if we trust in the Lord, He'll look out for us just like He did for Sarah."

"No matter what our husbands do." A voice agreed.

"Or don't do." Another one added.

"So are you saying we're not to trust our husbands?" A worried plea rose from the back.

"No," Clara said, "I think the Bible is saying we are to put our trust in the Lord—first."

Beatrice jumped back up to the podium. She tried to smile, but her face wouldn't play along. "Anyway," she said, sliding Clara aside. "We thank our sister, here, for her input. And next time, we'll get back to our original verses in Ephesians 5. Have a safe and happy

Christmas and New Year's season everyone. See you after the holidays."

As the ladies started milling around to leave, Beatrice mouthed to Jasmine, "Meet me in the back."

Jasmine joined Beatrice in the back of the room, but Clara remained in earshot. "Well, are you just too excited?" Beatrice strutted.

"About what?" Jasmine said, trying to appear nonchalant.

"About the New Year's Eve Ball, silly." Beatrice set her hands on her hip. "Didn't that Dex of yours tell you anything?" She swelled with pride. "My Harold invited me to be his date last night."

"Dex has been up to his neck in an important murder trial, Beatrice." Jasmine tried to outmaneuver her adversary. "I'm sure he'll get around to telling me when his workload calms down."

"Well, don't wait too long, Jasmine." Beatrice's nose flared. "I've checked around, and the costumes are going fast—"

"Costumes?" Jasmine squeaked, unable to mask her surprise.

"Oh, didn't I say?" Beatrice's eyes twinkled. She was delighted her husband had entrusted her with information that obviously Jasmine's had not. "It's a costume ball! Isn't that exciting?"

"Yes." Jasmine forced a smile. "Exciting." But she couldn't stop wondering why Dex hadn't mentioned it to her. Why she had to hear it from Beatrice, of all people? And wasn't New Year's Eve only three weeks away?

"Well, see you there!" Beatrice crowed. "Harold and I plan to set that Ball on its ear. We make a great team, you know." She exited with a flourish. "Ta-Ta."

"See you later, Jasmine." Clara waved. She'd been standing close enough to hear it all. "Have a blessed holiday, my sister."

"You, too, Clara." Jasmine winced. *I wonder if Abraham's Sarah had to go home alone.*

CHAPTER 18
Leeza

Leeza had Christmas dinner catered at her dad's house. He'd sounded a little weak the last time they spoke on the phone. Although her dad had protested, as expected, she'd made the arrangements anyway. "I want us to have a relaxing time together, Dad." She'd explained to him on one of their many calls. "I don't want you wrestling with a 20-pound turkey and sweating over a hot oven at Christmastime."

The house was filled with the festive smells of the season when Leeza arrived at her dad's home at noon, and she was glad for her decision to keep the preparations as simple as possible. "I'm here, Dad," she called as she turned her key in his lock.

"Come in, Sweet-Girl," her dad called in reply. "I'm here in the kitchen."

And so he was, wearing his oxygen mask between sips of hot cocoa. His wearing the face mask, instead of the simple cannula, usually signaled he was having a more difficult time breathing. And the dark circles under his baggy eyes confirmed it. "Want a cup?" He offered. "It's your favorite, the kind with marshmallows." He reminded her.

"Don't mind if I do," Leeza said jovially. "But sit. I'll get it myself."

"So how was your trip from New York?" Lee Manchester said.

"It's Christmas Day," Leeza said, "not so much traffic out there."

"Glad the snow held off, too." Lee said. "Seems like we'll have a white New Year's instead."

"Seems like," Leeza said agreeably as she brought over her cocoa to sit at the kitchen table with her dad.

"It's always good having you here, Leeza." Her dad nodded. "Reminds me of old times…good times…when it was just me and you."

"Yeah, Dad, I know." Leeza agreed, hoping he wouldn't start in again about their times in the kitchen alone, without her Mom. He liked remembering those times, but Leeza liked remembering the times when the three of them were together as a family. There were lots of those times, too.

"So how are things at work?" Her dad persisted.

"Dad, I was hoping we'd get into that after dinner." Leeza moaned. "I just want to sit here with you and enjoy Christmas Day."

"Tired, are you?" Her dad peered into her eyes. "What's the matter? What's going on?"

"Dad—" Leeza whined.

"We'll eat our dinner in peace, no matter." Lee Manchester pressed. "But tell me now what's got you so disturbed."

"I'm not disturbed." Leeza pushed back. "I've been traveling a lot, and I'm just tired. Major jet lag—"

"I know." Lee pursued. "Argentina and—"

"China, and Australia, and—"

"But that's nothing for you, Leeza." Her dad egged on. "You love to travel."

"Yes, Dad." Leeza was starting to get perturbed. "I love to travel for leisure, but this is far from leisure. This is work. And it is very hard work, Dad."

"I know that, Sweet-Girl, but this is what you've been groomed for; this is your life—"

"Is it?" Leeza fought to control her tone. "Is it, indeed?" she said. "Or do you forget I wanted to be a painter? And Mom supported my ambitions to be an artist—"

"That was rubbish!" Her dad sucked for air. "This is the real world! I sent you to all the best schools. I made sure you had every advantage, for just this sort of challenge."

"But that doesn't make it any easier, Dad; especially with the added pressure of time." Leeza stated emphatically. "I have less than three months to get these three, new blue-chip clients signed up, remember?"

"But there's no pressure." Her dad wheezed excitedly. "From what you've told me, you have one, new blue-chipper, and that boy...Kyle...has one. So you're evenly matched for the moment." Lee's oxygen tank pumped fiercely. "But not for long, for you will trounce that silly boy in the end. I'm sure of it!"

Leeza lowered her head to regain her composure. This is not the conversation she'd planned for on Christmas Day; her only day off for over a month. "Dad," she said through clenched teeth, "that is not the situation at all. And if it is all right with you, I'd rather reserve this conversation until after we've enjoyed this wonderful meal together." She forced a smile. "These delicious smells are killing me."

"The food can wait!" Her dad gasped, and the compressor whooshed to give him more air. "I need to know what's going on with this—this contest between you and Kyle." He sucked for wind. "Don't you understand, Leeza? It will make all the difference in the success of your career!"

"Yes, Dad, I understand!" Leeza blared back. "But talking about it with you now will not make any difference in the outcome. But having a quiet, relaxing meal with you just might."

"What are the chances of that?" Lee Manchester protested. "I need to know what's going on, and I need to know right this minute!"

"Okay!" Leeza stood up from the table and emptied her half cup of cocoa into the sink. "Have it your way, Dad. You always do!"

"So then," her dad said more quietly. "Please, Sweet-Girl, sit back down and tell me what I need to know."

"It's not what you think, Dad."

"So tell me."

"Mr. Cole let it slip—"

"What? What?"

"I have one, new blue-chip client from Argentina—"

"Yes. Yes."

"But Kyle has two—"

"Two?" Lee Manchester wheezed. "Leeza, how could you let this happen?"

"Let this happen?" Leeza blew. "I didn't let it happen, Dad. Kyle is courting U.S. companies. But me, I've got to fly all over the world trying to get my three new clients—"

"But is that fair?" Lee questioned.

"Fair, or not, Dad, that's the way it is." Leeza snapped. "Kyle had first dibs at Mr. Cole's secret list, and he picked all of the American companies to go after. That left me with the international trade." She huffed. "That's just the way it is; and regardless of the disadvantage, I still need to be the first to get my three, new firms to beat out Kyle."

"And you will!" Her dad cheered. "You will beat out this, Kyle. He can't hold a candle to my Sweet-Girl."

Leeza breathed deep and long. "Whatever, Dad—"

"That attitude will not get you there, Leeza!" Her dad said sharply. "You've got to put your back into this! You've got to take off the kid gloves and play hard ball if you want to win this, Leeza! You've got to double-down, get in there and beat him at his own game; beat the pants off that Kyle!" Lee's oxygen mask was fogging up. "Kyle's got the balls and brute force, but you've got the breeding, the skill, the finesse, the beauty…and not to mention, your feminine charm—"

"Dad, what are you saying?" Leeza's mouth gaped.

"You've got to use everything you've got, Leeza." Her dad panted. "Lay it all on the line."

"Dad, are you saying what I think you're saying?" Leeza's mind immediately raced to Brandi and her dirty tricks—sleeping with the partner, cheating, stealing, double-dealing, anything, and everything to win.

Her dad's eyes gleamed lecherously over his face mask. "You know what I'm saying, Leeza." He wheezed. "This is not the time to be squeamish. This is not the time to hold back." He pressed his point. "This is the time to pull out all the stops. This is the time to seize the day! That's how you'll outstrip that Kyle. Use all your assets!"

"But Dad—"

Lee coughed and fought to breathe. "Leeza, you'll only be disappointed if you don't do this. I've sacrificed far too much for you to get to this point. Everything I've done is riding on this!"

"That's it, isn't it, Dad?" Leeza pushed back from the table. She was near tears. "It always comes back to you, and what you've done for me. Well, I'll have you know I'm doing my very best. And that's all I can do!"

"Then your best had better be good enough." Lee Manchester was near collapse. "Because everything—you hear me—everything is riding on this!"

"I'd better go, Dad." Leeza leapt up from her chair. "So you can calm down and get some rest."

Lee could only raise one hand in surrender; he was too winded to speak.

"I'll get you settled in, Dad, and I'll pack the food away so you can get to it later." Leeza managed to give him a kiss on the cheek. "I do love you, Dad," she said, "and rest assured, I'm doing my very best."

CHAPTER 19
Cristal

Nearly thirty days had passed since Cristal's last uninvited visit to her mother's home on Thanksgiving Day. During their subsequent chats, Cristal hadn't let on to her sister or her mother that she'd spied out their little clandestine Thanksgiving feast. Since neither Chanel nor Chantilly had come clean, Cristal didn't want to admit how much their lie had hurt her. She'd kept up a brave front and acted like she suspected nothing. There was no way she wanted to give them the satisfaction of knowing they had caused her such great misery.

But this time, she and Malik were invited guests to Chantilly's annual Christmas brunch. "It's Christmas, Babe. Let's just put it in the past," Cristal said when she told Malik she'd accepted Chantilly's invitation for the two of them. He fumed a bit, but didn't disagree. "Besides," Cristal said, "she's invited all our Georgia cousins up from Macon and Warner Robins, and I haven't seen them since Daddy's funeral. Maybe she's trying to make up for dissing me at Thanksgiving, huh? Anyhow, it'll be good for us all to get together again; although, it will make me miss Daddy that much more."

Malik drove Cristal's red Cadillac STS, in keeping with the season. As they crunched up the white, cobble-stoned driveway to Chantilly's mansion, the scene was a majestic wonderland. All along the way, everything was glamour and glitz. The trees and sculptured shrubs were lit up with festive lights and holiday sparkle. There was the mixed message of animated snowmen singing secular carols, alongside life-sized trumpeting angels and giant candy-striped lollipops. The elaborate menagerie culminated near the garage with a huge inflated Santa and a deluxe bounce castle, flags included. But despite the warm car and the extravagant surroundings on this cool, crisp morning, Cristal was shrinking deeper into her seat.

"You okay?" Malik said.

"I'm good." Cristal squirmed. "Just can't shake off the last time I was here. Trying not to feel some kinda way bout that." She shrank deeper into her seat. "They've called me on the phone about this-that-and-the-other since Thanksgiving, but neither one of them has 'fessed up about leaving me out."

"This was your idea," Malik said. "We can turn around right now if you want to."

"Nope." Cristal's grey eyes brightened. "I'm bigger than that…and it's Christmas. Don't you just love this season, Malik." She cuddled closer to him.

"I sure do," he said and smoothed her mocha skin with his hand, "especially when my baby has a smile on her face."

"Oh, Malik," she cooed, "I do love you so."

"Ditto." He kissed her gently on her ruby lips.

When they reached the door, Cristal was bundled up tightly in her white mink jacket, leather caramel-colored skinny jeans with matching boots and cashmere sweater. Malik was sporting a black leather bomber over a grey wool sweater and slacks. His scarf and cap, gray/black tweed, had been a surprise gift from Cristal. They looked quite the prosperous couple.

"Top of the morning to you—Sir, Madam." Willie, the hired butler for the occasion, greeted them at the door.

Chanel glared at them from across the room and headed in their direction. Travis Johnson, who had just arrived, was standing inside the foyer, as well. He gave Cristal and Malik a warm hug. "Merry Christmas, Uncle Travis." Cristal smiled as Malik handed off their coats to the butler, along with a huge bag of gifts to be added under the sparkling, floor-to-ceiling Christmas tree. "I'm so happy you could make it." She beamed. Travis Johnson could best be described as tall, dark and handsome, with a thick head of hair that curled at his temples. He wasn't really her uncle, but he had been her daddy's best friend since grade school, the family's lawyer, and her godfather of record. She and Chanel had called him Uncle Travis from the time they were big enough to get horsey rides on his knee.

"Hello, Uncle Travis." Chanel offered him air kisses. And her lips curled disdainfully when she added, "Sis, Malik." She whisked them off to the dining room where Chantilly was sitting in judgment at the head of the mile-long black lacquered table. "Look who's here, Mother," Chanel announced, sounding like a dutiful court jester.

"Oh, hello there." Chantilly granted sparingly. "Glad you could join us; and you, too, Travis." She looked down at her diamond encrusted Rolex. "On time for a change."

"And Merry Christmas to you, too," Travis said, and the warmth of his smile brightened up the room.

"Hello, Mother." Cristal smiled. "Thanks for the invite. I sure am looking forward to seeing the whole Georgia clan." Malik offered a nod in Chantilly's direction, but said nothing.

"Your cousins from Macon and Warner Robins have been trickling in." Chantilly sniffed. "It's just like that side of the family to act like country Georgia folk...never on time." She waved off Cristal's attempt to kiss her cheek. "But I hope you're happy. These are your daddy's people, dear, not mine."

Malik moved toward the beverage center and turned to Cristal. "Something to drink, Babe?" Cristal waved her hand to decline. "How about you, Uncle Travis?" He politely declined.

"So is Uncle Blaze here, yet?" Cristal pursued her line of questioning. "And Aunt Florina?"

"Not yet." Chanel hazarded a reply when she saw Chantilly had no intention of responding to Cristal. "But let's go into the great room and see who is here, shall we?" Chanel led the way, and Cristal and Malik followed. He had no desire to be in the same room with Chantilly Moore. He'd leave that thankless chore to Uncle Travis.

Just then, there was a ruckus at the front door. "Hey y'all!" came the deep baritone of Uncle Blaze surrounded by the constant chirping and cackling of Aunt Florina. They always made the same raucous entrance, like they'd practiced their timing before they left the car. "Come here, Gal." Uncle Blaze grabbed Cristal by the arm and pulled her toward him. "You done got to be a fine young thang, ain't ya?" he said.

"Fine; yes, fine young thang." Aunt Florina echoed in stereo.

Chanel stood far enough away so this bear of a man couldn't lay one of his giant paws on her. But Cristal gave each of them a big hug and smiled like the sun had been cranked up to high. "It's so good to see you Uncle Blaze, Aunt Florina."

"Good to see you, too, Cristal," Uncle Blaze said. "You've always been my favorite." His eyes burned into Chanel's back as she made a hasty retreat to the other side of the room. "Not like your stuck-up sister over there."

"Yeah. Stuck-up. Stuck-up." Aunt Florina intoned.

"You remember Malik, right?" Cristal refocused their attention.

"Remember?" Uncle Blaze blared. "Who could forget a lucky man like this?"

"Yes, lucky man; lucky man." Aunt Florina chortled. Florina had no doubt been a looker in her day, but now there were a few slats missing in her picket-fence smile.

"He's the one what gets to sleep with my pretty little niece every night." Uncle Blaze roared, and Aunt Florina did the same. "Can't nobody forget you, Man!" He punched Malik in the shoulder.

It's gonna be on—up in here—up in here! Malik smiled to himself as he recalled the family history that Cristal had shared with him over the years. It seems her daddy, Morgan Moore, was one of six sons—the youngest and the only light-skinned one of the bunch.

All of the six sons had one son, except for her daddy who had two daughters. And Uncle Blaze was the last living brother. Evidently, their family had grown up in Macon, a stone's throw from the Warner Robins Air Force Base, where their daddy and most of his clan worked. When Morgan Moore joined the Air Force, he ended up at the base in Warner Robins, where he retired to attend college at Mercer University in Macon. He studied engineering and became a celebrated engineer for the B & E Railroad. So much so, that before his untimely passing, the railroad named a container facility in his honor. Mercer is also where he'd met and married Chantilly, and the rest is history. Morgan had invested his money well and made a killing in the stock market. He died in 2007, before the Wall Street meltdown. But Chantilly had already moved all of his considerable holdings into cash before the stock crash. Smart move on her part, considering. But his brothers were not as interested in attending college or bettering their station in life, so they were the other side of the family. But to his credit, until the day he died, Morgan kept close ties with all his family; even though it chapped Chantilly's hide to be around what she so unaffectionately referred to as 'his country bumpkin cousins'—John *Blaze* Moore and his wife, Florina, heading up the hit parade.

In the great room, there were four other couples and Cousin Bay-Ray, who always seemed to travel solo. Some said he was gay, but nobody asked because nobody really wanted to know. When Blaze and Florina entered the beautifully appointed room filled with festive holiday cheer, they all stood up in reverence. "Hey, y'all." Uncle Blaze blared heartily. "Glad y'all made it up here in one piece."

"Yeah, in one piece." Aunt Florina chirped.

Everybody shook hands and hugged like they were seeing each other for the first time. Cristal greeted them all, pulling Malik in tow. Chanel was not the least bit interested in this family scene. She filtered back into the dining room with Chantilly and Uncle Travis.

Cousin Elmo, Blaze's son, had a new girlfriend with him since the last time. She had a bra on so tight, it was pushing up her buxom bosom to her chin, and there was something tattooed across her cleavage. Malik couldn't quite make it out so he moved in a little closer, while Elmo was introducing his date to Cristal. Elmo spoke with a sense of pride when he said, "This here is Lucinda Lovely."

"She is lovely." Cristal took in her red velvet dress that stopped mid-thigh over black fishnets. The silver rhinestone shoes were an extra added touch.

"Don't y'all listen to him," she drawled. "My name is really Lucinda Lewis." She giggled. "Elmo know Lovely just my stage name."

"Stage?" Cristal's brows rose warily. "And what stage might that be?"

"I'm a stripper," Lucinda said nonchalantly, "down at the Wet & Slippery Gentlemen's Club in Warner Robins."

"Oh?" Cristal said as Malik was leading her away. In the process he was able to read the tattoo across her chest. It read, "Big Guns."

The other couples hugged Cristal and told her how much they missed her daddy. They were misting up to varying degrees when the butler entered the great room. "Brunch is served," he said in a haughty tone, and everybody gave him a blank stare. Finally, he cleared his throat and repeated it Atlanta-style, "It's time to get yo grub on, y'all." To which, everyone loosened up and began to move toward the dining room.

"Take your places at your assigned seats, please." Chantilly called from the head of the table. Her bright skin was radiant under the warm glow of the chandelier. And with the addition of Uncle Travis—Chantilly, Chanel and her husband, Denver—were the only three of lighter hue at the table set for seventeen. Chanel's four, bright-faced cherubs had been resigned to the kiddie table in the kitchen with the butler.

"You'll find your name on the gold-embossed place cards." Chantilly droned on with instructions as her guests found their seats with ease. Blaze and Florina had been assigned the seats furthest away from Chantilly. She'd made sure of that. "It's so good to see all of you." Chantilly postured. "If only my dear Morgan could be here to see this." All heads snatched toward Chantilly. Her feeble attempt at sentimentality was totally out of character. Besides, the man had been dead, now, going on seven years, and this was their first time hearing from the woman.

In an attempt to lighten the mood, Uncle Blaze said, "And we mighty glad you invited us all up here, too, Chantilly." He grinned wide. "Mighty white o' ya."

"Yeah, mighty white!" They all grinned and cackled along with Aunt Florina.

"Your food will be served by Willie, but you can obtain your own beverages from the beverage station." Chantilly pointed to the slick, black lacquered bar. "There's egg nog, with a little kick." Chantilly pursed her lips. "Also, wine and champagne." She explained. "Ahh, here's Willie with our first course. Eat up everyone and enjoy!"

"Isn't anybody gonna pray?" Malik knifed in.

"Well, since it's your idea, Malik," Chantilly said grandly, "you do the honors."

And he did. "Lord, thank you for this bounty and this family that has gathered together to celebrate the miracle of Your birth. Please, Lord, bless us, now, each and every one, in Jesus' name. Amen."

"Amen." They chorused.

Cousin Bay-Ray made his way to the beverage center a number of times while they were threading doubtful spoons through the first course of vichyssoise—a cold, creamy soup concoction. *Cold soup on a cold day? What the heck?*

But nobody really noticed Bay-Ray because the conversation was ripe between Elmo and Lucinda. She was telling him and everyone in ear shot—whether they wanted to hear or not—about her rich clientele from the Warner Robins Air Force Base—in all its graphic detail. "Sergeant Tee-Roy may be on the short side," she said, "but what's in his wallet is as big as what's in his pants—"

"Oh, my God!" Chantilly's face flamed beet red, chin to forehead, because she'd made the unfortunate choice of seating the couple closest to her.

By the time the second course was served, salade niçoise, and everybody had set about picking out the anchovies, Cousin Bay-Ray's face hit the gold-rimmed china plate with a loud crash. Chantilly jumped up, and Uncle Blaze moved around the table to see what had happened.

"Bay-Ray!" Blaze pulled the wild greens off his narrow chin and smacked his sunken cheeks. "Bay-Ray, what wrong with you, boy?"

"Ugh-ugh," was all Bay-Ray could manage. But everybody was relieved to hear he was still alive.

Blaze picked up his glass and gave it a deep sniff. "This boy, here, drunk. That what be the matter."

"Drunk?" Chantilly hoped up, blue veins popping in her neck. "How is that possible? For this very reason, I only served the egg nog and the wines."

"Don't know 'bout that." Blaze cajoled. "But this here boy is drunk as a skunk. He be reeking with liquor."

Chantilly moved over and looked under the bar where she'd stashed the good stuff. "Here's the problem." She seethed. "That…cousin of yours has broken the seal on my top-shelf bourbon *and* my top-shelf vodka. He's been sneaking drinks!"

"Is that so?" Uncle Blaze's eyes burned into Chantilly. They were probably the reason for his enduring nickname.

"And he mighta started in on his daily dose o' moonshine 'fore he got here." Aunt Florina squeaked.

"But be that as it may," Uncle Blaze said, "the boy here be drunk. So what we gonna do with him?"

"Put him upstairs…in the attic bedroom." Chantilly pointed. "Come on, Elmo. Gimme a hand 'cause he out."

Uncle Travis rose. "May I be of assistance?" He offered.

"Naw," Uncle Blaze said, "me and Elmo, here, we got this. Ain't no need for you to get your suit all wrankled—"

"Or throwed-up on." Elmo added. "It's like this with Bay-Ray everywhere we go."

"Can't take the boy nowhere." Florina chipped in.

Chantilly eyed Chanel to follow the men to be sure they didn't go into any of the other upstairs bedrooms where she kept her valuables. Although Chanel's husband, Denver, was seated at her side, he didn't make a move. He'd learned not to stir in this house unless he was expressly asked to do so.

"Cristal," Chantilly said, "these are your people! I brought them here as a gift to you since you were your daddy's favorite. You look like them," she said, referring to Cristal's darker hue. "You act like them. And I'm holding you accountable for this!"

Cristal shrank into herself. Everyone watched as she melted away like a marshmallow before their very eyes.

"Hold on there!" Malik spoke up in her defense. "You don't get to talk to my wife like that."

"Chantilly, this is uncalled for." Uncle Travis pleaded. "There's no reason for you to speak to your daughter in that tone."

"The operative word being, *my* daughter." Chantilly shook her finger at Uncle Travis. "You, on the other hand, are an invited guest." She glared at him wildly. "And for all those who're staying, it's time for us to get back to this lovely meal."

Uncle Travis tossed his gold-edged napkin onto the table. "Minus one," he said, pushing back his chair. He rose, back straight, and strode to the door. "Merry Christmas, everyone."

Malik looked at Cristal, but her misty eyes were pleading with him to stay. Hand trembling, she picked up her salad fork, and he followed suit. The rest of the family picked up their conversations where they'd left off. They were used to Bay-Ray's mess. And they never understood a word coming out of Chantilly's mouth anyhow— with her *'high-siding self'*. Besides, the duck l'orange and standing rib roast would be well worth the wait.

CHAPTER 20
Jasmine

Christmas was a heavy affair. Jasmine had plodded through the month of December like a shadow. In times past, the holidays had been an exciting time of year. She and Madeline would put up the tree, and shop for special ornaments and gifts. They would have lights and glitter everywhere. And Jasmine looked forward to seeing the excitement on their faces when they all gathered around to open their presents. They would always eat too much of the soul food she prepared and OD on football and board games.

But this year would be different. Madeline was not coming home this year. And even though Dex had won his precious Dunston case, he didn't seem any happier for the victory. He drifted in and out of the house, night and day, on one pretense or the other. It was driving Jasmine mad, and she knew it. Her hair was falling out. Plugs of it were coming out in her afro pick. Her skin was looking drab and old, and her clothes hung on her like they belonged to someone else. Her nerves were frayed down to the quick. She was a wreck. It occurred to her that the old folk in her charge were making a better go of it this holiday than she was; especially, the old guys who pinched her butt every time she made her rounds on the geriatric ward at Parkland Hospital.

Jasmine even found herself siding with Dex. *What man in his right mind would want to come home to me?* Thanksgiving without Dex and Madeline had been so lonely and disappointing, but Christmas Day promised to be better. At least Dex would be home; and to that extent, they'd be a family.

Dex was already snoring by the time Jasmine reached their bedroom around 9 p.m. on Christmas Eve. But she put on the new, silk nighty she'd bought for the occasion anyway. She curled up as close to his warm body as she could and slept soundly for a change.

But she rose up early to make Dex's favorites for breakfast. She hummed in the kitchen as she prepared heart-shaped pancakes, hot syrup and loads of crisp bacon. Dex stumbled down to the kitchen in his black flannel robe and slippers when Jasmine called him to the table.

"Something smells good," Dex said as his nose led him into the kitchen. "You're up mighty early, Jazz."

"Just wanted to make the day special for you, Dex." She brightened. "It's Christmas!"

"And so it is." Dex kissed her on the cheek and Jasmine snuggled against his neck.

"I thought you'd wait up for me last night." She cooed. "I had something special for you then, too."

Dex coughed. "Oh, you know how it is, Jazz." He moved away from her to pour coffee into their gold-rimmed cups. "With all the pressure at work these days, sometimes my ED kicks in."

Jasmine's eyes bucked. "You—Dexter Davis—erectile dysfunction?"

"I'm a man, aren't I?" Dex said defensively. "It happens."

"Sure," Jasmine said, stifling her next remark about the times he'd rocked her world all night long. Back then, her head banging against the headboard and their moans of ecstasy had been a nightly affair. But that was then, and this was now; and she didn't want to spoil the mood. "Go settle yourself in the dining room," she said, "and I'll serve you in there."

"Thanks, Hon." Dex moved out, china cups in hand.

Jasmine dished up the food on platters and brought them into the dining room for a special treat. She had the table set with all her finest dishes and candles. She even poured their orange juice into crystal goblets. Dex had taken a seat at the head of the table, and she sat beside him.

Jasmine asked the blessing. "Lord, thank you for the miracle of your birth and letting us share it on this day…together. I pray that You will also keep Madeline safe and happy, today and every day. And please bless the Ambassador and his family. Bless this food to our use, and us to your service. Amen."

Dex's jaws were locked when Jasmine lifted her head. "You couldn't do it, could you, Jazz?" he said. "You couldn't let it go about me allowing Madeline to spend the holidays in Nigeria with Imani and her family?"

"I didn't—"

"We've had this out several times already, but you had to dig at me again, even in your prayers." Dex bristled.

"I'm not digging at you, Dex—"

"Enough." Dex slapped pancakes and bacon onto his plate. He took a large gulp of orange juice.

Jasmine excused herself to get more coffee. Her hand was trembling so badly she could hardly pour. When she returned, a blue box with a brightly-colored bow was at her place. "What's this?" She puzzled.

"It's your gift." Dex poured more hot syrup on his pancakes. "Merry Christmas."

"But I put yours under the tree."

"So." Dex simmered. "Open it. It's yours. I'll get mine later."

Jasmine's china cup rattled into its saucer. Her twitchy fingers worked the bow off the box. "My goodness!" Jasmine gasped when she removed the lid. "Dex!" was all she could say. Inside, laid a pair of diamond earrings and a diamond-studded tennis bracelet. They were a perfect match to the Rolex watch he'd given her for their 25th wedding anniversary in June. "Oh, what a nice surprise!"

"Nice?" Dex peered at her. "Is that all you can say?"

Jasmine got up and put her arms around his neck where he sat. "It's fabulous, Dex!" she said, laying it on thick. "I just never expected anything this nice, so soon after our anniversary!" She tried to kiss his lips, but he offered her his cheek instead.

"You're my wife." Dex rumbled. "My wife deserves nice things. You're looking at over five carats of diamonds there."

Jasmine pulled her gifts out of their nesting place and put them on. She flew to the floor-to-ceiling mirror on the dining room wall to look them over. She didn't like what she saw. The earrings were long and gorgeous; the tennis bracelet bright and shiny, but she was not. She looked like a broken doll, all dressed up with nowhere to go.

"You like?" Dex said proudly.

Jasmine dribbled back into her chair and nibbled on a piece of bacon. "You have exquisite taste, Dex," she said. "This is a beautiful gift." But she knew it was more to prove he was a big man than out of any genuine love for her.

"Well, don't be so cheerful about it." Dex scolded. "You sound like you just lost your best friend."

"I was just thinking nobody will get a chance to see them at the costume ball," Jasmine said, trying to mask her true feelings.

"Costume ball?" Dex's face creased. "What costume ball?"

"The Bar Association's New Year's Eve Ball." Jasmine shrugged. "Beatrice Garner told me about it at our last Bible Study."

"That fake, donkey-faced woman!" Dex tossed his cloth napkin into his syrupy plate. "What does she know about anything?"

"She knows her husband, Harold, invited her to the Ball." Jasmine braced herself for the tidal wave cresting in Dex's eyes. "You know him. He's a defense attorney like you, remember?"

"Sure. I know Horrible Harold, but what's that got to do with you?"

"His wife says there's going to be a costume ball on New Year's Eve…and everyone is invited." Jasmine tried to minimize his guilt. "And I know you've been really busy, so I picked us out some costumes before they were all gone." She forced a smile. "We're going as Batman and Robin."

"We're not going as anything!" Dex pushed back his chair. "You're not going!"

"What do you mean, I'm not going?" Jasmine's belly seized. "You said you needed all the brownie points you can get. This is an important event. Everyone who's anyone will be there and—"

"But you won't be there." Dex blared. "Not with me."

"Dex, I don't understand," Jasmine said softly, trying to diffuse his anger.

"I am not inviting you to go to the New Year's Eve Ball with me," Dex said one word at a time. "Get it?"

"I hear you." Jasmine fought back her tears. "But I don't understand."

"If I go," Dex said, "I want to be free to mix and mingle—"

"But I won't stop you—"

"Wanna know what I gave Madi for Christmas?" Dex spun the conversation on its ear to stifle Jasmine's objections to the Ball and to show her once again who was boss.

"What?" Jasmine said, so confused she was dizzy. "What did you give Madeline?"

"Her grades are good...excellent in fact."

"Yes." Jasmine agreed. "I'm very proud—"

"So I gave her my permission to travel with Ambassador Acho and his family to Hawaii for Spring Break." He preened. "And I'm footing the bill."

"You did what?" Jasmine's mind whirled recklessly.

"You heard me." Dex stuck out his chest. "It will be the first time the Ambassador will be visiting the Big Island, and Imani wants Madeline to go with her. Great opportunity, huh?"

"Dex, are you losing your mind?" Jasmine said, but it was her mind that she was afraid was at risk. "I've not seen our daughter since September; since I took her to D.C. Instead of coming home, you've let her spend every holiday with the Ambassador's family." Jasmine's hot tears began to trail down her cheeks. "I want to see my baby!"

"That's just it!" Dex retorted. "Madi is not your baby. She's a very capable young woman who doesn't want you smothering her anymore."

"Smothering her?" Jasmine cried. "I love her!"

"Same thing." Dex sniped. "I, on the other hand, want Madeline to have every advantage to broaden her future—"

"Broadening her future doesn't mean abandoning her family!" Jasmine wailed. "I miss Madeline. You don't miss her because you're never home." Her words spilled over before she could catch them.

"Is that right, Jazz? Are you equating my presence or absence in this horrible house with my love for my daughter?" Dex's face pulsed in wild shades of blue. "Well, let me set the record straight. I love my daughter! It's you I can't stand!" He stormed out of the dining room and stomped his way upstairs. "I'm moving into the guest room, and you needn't concern yourself anymore with my goings and comings." He screamed. "Hope that makes you happy, Jasmine!"

CHAPTER 21
Leeza

"Thank you for agreeing to see me, Mr. Cole," Leeza said coolly. Unlike their last encounter, this time she'd followed protocol and made an appointment through his secretary.

"But, of course, Miss Manchester." Dick Cole sat down his stained coffee mug. "I hope this means you have some good news for me." He looked back at the clock on his credenza. The mini Christmas tree had been removed, and the empty spot signaled his hopes for the New Year, when he could vacate this office for his new digs in the Partner's Suite.

"And I hope you have some good news for me as well, sir," Leeza said coyly."

"What on earth do you mean?" Dick Cole stared blankly.

"Well, the last time I was in your office, I got the unfortunate news that Kyle was ahead of me two-to-one in our quest to attract new super clients for your roster." Leeza moved cautiously. "And I hope this time I won't hear that Kyle has three new clients, which would mean all bets are off and Kyle has bested me in our little contest."

"What are you holding back from me, Leeza?" Cole snapped. This was not a game he was willing to play. Whether Kyle had beat her or not, he wanted each of them to bring him as many new, blue-chip clients as possible to bolster his chances at partner. "So come out with it, and say what you have to say." He growled. "I have some pressing appointments this afternoon."

"I think it only fair that you go first, sir." Leeza had learned from their last encounter that her exuberance didn't always play well in the confines of his cut-throat domain. And she wasn't about to give him anything else without getting something in return.

"Well, all right." Cole conceded warily. "If you're asking me if Kyle has already signed-on his three, new clients, the answer is no—not yet. He's working feverishly, of course, as I'm sure you are, too; but he has not reached the magic number, three. He has not won the victory…not yet."

"All right then." Leeza granted. "I guess my news is noteworthy."

"What is your news, Miss Manchester?" The stray hair atop Cole's head was standing at attention.

Leeza made a little clapping sound with her hands; something attending to a drum roll. "Well, then, Mr. Cole, I guess you'll be glad to know that I have signed-on my second, new blue chipper!"

"Really?" Cole tried to conceal his delight, but he was having a difficult time pulling it off. "And who might that be, Miss Manchester?"

Leeza grew more comfortable in her guest chair. "Well, you remember the Chinese firm I signed-on back in late summer—the one in Beijing?"

"Zhang Wei International?" Cole rolled his hand for her to continue. "Yes-Yes."

"As a follow-up courtesy," Leeza said, "I called Mrs. Zhang Wei, his wife, to wish her and her family a Happy New Year—"

"And—"

"And." Leeza droned on. "And we got to talking about the people we knew and the contacts I was pursuing." She smiled slyly. "And as it turned out, Mamie Zhang Wei, is very good friends with Mrs. Enez Burgerstrom—"

"The wife of Lars Burgerstrom of Salinger Industries?"

"Yes!" Leeza exclaimed. No longer able to keep her cool. "And she made the overtures with Mrs. Burgerstrom for me—"

"Go on—"

"And long story short." Leeza smiled. "I was invited to Sweden for an International Women's Brunch that Mrs. Burgerstrom was hosting as a fundraiser for her latest cause. And we hit it off, just like that!"

"Wonderful!" Dick Cole was hanging on her every word.

"And the next thing I knew Enez had me meeting with her husband's COO, and then the CEO and CFO, and finally Mr. Burgerstrom himself. After that, we cut the deal in record time. I signed-up Salinger Industries that day in fact." Leeza bragged. "See what good connections will do. It's our lifeblood in this crazy business. Never know when who you meet will get you the business."

Dick Cole rubbed his hands together like a greedy land baron who'd just stolen the last widow's ranch. "This is stupendous, Miss Manchester!" His excitement caught in his throat. "You have two, new blue chippers; Kyle has two. I should've pitted you two against each other years ago. I might've made partner that much sooner."

Leeza's face dropped. The idea that Cole could only think of his own success at a time like this was rather disheartening. But she played along. "Well, there you have it, Mr. Cole," she said. "Kyle and I are neck and neck, and you have four new clients to crow about."

"And crow I will...in March." Cole added quickly. "I hope you and Kyle will keep your success under your hats until I have the opportunity to make the big, public splash right before the Partner's Selection Panel kicks off." He impaled her with his eyes. "I hope you understand the importance of timing as it relates to breaking this news. I'm going to drop it on them like a bombshell."

"I understand." Leeza swirled her lips disdainfully. "But I don't know about Kyle."

"Don't worry about Kyle." Cole sniffed. "His head was about to blow off his shoulders because he wanted to shout it to the whole office, but I've sworn him to secrecy until after my meeting with the Partner's Selection Panel in March."

Leeza rose from her chair. "Then I guess I'll go and let you get on with your day, sir."

"Sit." Cole jabbed his finger at Leeza to halt her departure. "Right now, you're running neck-and-neck with our ballsy Mr. Kyle Leary," he said to keep up the pressure. "But…just between me and you, my money's on you to win this little contest."

Leeza bobbled back into her chair. "Why's that, sir," she said, mystified by his sudden change of heart.

"As you know, Miss Manchester," Cole hummed in a low whisper, "Kyle picked all of the North American companies on my list, which was a smart move on his part." He laced his fingers together. "But it also means that his final prospect is the Fairchild Group."

"Yes, I figured as much." Leeza granted. "They're tough—"

"My point, exactly." Cole took a long sip of his stale coffee. "And I don't think Kyle has the juice to get in with the Fairchilds. They're a snobbish bunch. They've got more Ivy Leaguers on board than a Harvard lacrosse team." Cole snorted. "That organization has no less than 25 gatekeepers, each one more proficient than the next. And their sole purpose is to keep newcomers like Kyle Leary, out. I'm afraid he doesn't have the breeding for the task."

"Yes, sir," Leeza said quietly, letting Cole tell the story.

"And it's too late for Kyle to go after an international firm." Cole slapped his desk deliberately. "So my money is on you, Miss Manchester. If you can find some way to land one more European firm, I suspect you'll be the grand prize winner of our little contest. And you know what that means—"

"Yes, sir, Boss." Leeza teased. "You—Mr. Richard *Dick* Cole— will become the newest partner at Bradford & Baker, Inc., and I will become the new Mr. Cole—"

"It means," Cole quickly clarified, "that I will take five, new blue chippers into the Partner's Selection Panel for my final interview." He snickered. "And I must admit, I'm going to enjoy beating the socks off that Dan Skinner, whether they're silk argyle, or not."

At that moment, Leeza realized Cole was only interested in his own future, and there would be another long night of painting away her frustrations in hers.

CHAPTER 22
Cristal

It was a cold New Year's Eve in Atlanta, and Chanel's eyes were looking out pass the intricate lace pattern of icicles forming on the windowpane in her old bedroom at her mother's house. She couldn't see a thing for the silent tears that were flowing down her cheeks when Cristal burst in, worked up into a lather. "You get up from there!" Cristal shouted at her sister. "You've got kids to raise!"

Chanel turned her vague, gray eyes. "Cristal?" She clutched at her nappy robe.

"Yes, Cristal!" She set her hands on her curvy hips. "Mother called me and told me you haven't been out of this room for two days." Cristal scanned the stuffy room. It was a place she'd rarely set foot in when they were growing up. Although they were only a year apart, Chanel had locked Cristal out of her bedroom for most of their childhood, with their mother's full permission.

"What do you want?" Chanel croaked in a voice so faint it was barely recognizable.

"C'mon, Chanel; snap out of it." Cristal said more compassionately this time, although she wanted to grab her and shake some sense into her. "Your kids are downstairs, and they need you."

"He's gone for good this time." Chanel cleared away the frog in her throat. "He's gone for good—"

"This time?" Cristal quizzed. "What'cha mean, this time?"

Chanel set her face to the window and her back to Cristal. "Did you know Denver was going to leave me a year into our marriage?" she mumbled.

"What?" Cristal frowned.

"But I got pregnant." Chanel confided. "In fact, I got pregnant every time he threatened to leave me." She breathed a rye chuckle. "Three times—four babies; the last time twins."

"But why?" Cristal shook her head. "Why would you let him hold you hostage like that?"

"What else could I do, Cris?" Chanel said weakly. "I have no money, no skills. I'm just a mother, and not a very good one at that. I'm nothing—"

"Chanel, that's not true." Cristal's voice softened.

"I am nothing." Chanel repeated. "I'm hollow inside. I gave him all of me…my self-respect…my power—"

"Is that what Denver wanted from you?" Cristal bristled, ready to box his ears.

"Nobody ever asks you to give up your power," Chanel whispered. "You do it because you feel like you have no choice. You've got to hold onto the relationship—at all cost. You can't risk letting it run its natural course. You can't afford to lose—"

"But I don't get it!" Cristal flared.

"Don't you see?" Chanel stiffened. "I got pregnant because Denver could leave me, but he couldn't leave his unborn child—"

"But why did he want to leave you in the first place?" Cristal whispered. "I thought y'all were so happy—the perfect couple."

"Because…he's always loved you." Chanel turned her sad eyes to face her sister. "Don't you see the way he still looks at you?"

"Me?" Cristal blared. "True; I met the man first, and maybe I led him on a little, but I never really liked him." Cristal waved her hands. "He too…light in the pants for me." This was her word for too cute, too soft guys. "And when I brought him home, you liked him; you married him; you had his babies. That was fine by me."

"I know that." Chanel admitted grudgingly, her voice gaining ground. "But that didn't stop him from loving…the image of you…and being envious of what you and Malik have."

"Talk to me, Girl," Cristal's eyes bucked. "'Cause I'm not getting this. Y'all got it all—"

"Except for one thing—" Chanel's voice choked.

"What?"

"Each other." Chanel shifted toward Cristal from the window seat. "Denver wants what you and Malik have...passion." She winced as though she were being crushed under the weight of her own admission. "But he says he could never find that with me. Denver says I'm incapable of deep feelings, or caring about anybody but myself." A weak smile flickered across the pained landscape of her face. "He says you're...so real, so true, so down. And me...I'm so plastic, so cold, so fake. He says I'm just like Chantilly."

"Oh, I see." Cristal diverted her eyes from the pain that had etched dark lines across her sister's pale skin.

"Do you really?" Chanel's voice shook. "Denver says he cannot bring in another New Year with me—live this lie another minute. He says it hit him square in the face when we were all here at Christmas brunch. He can't stand being around you—and Malik—seeing the love you share. He can't stand being around Mother—hating on you and doting on me. He can't stand being around me...and he says he can't fake it any longer." Her head drooped pitifully.

"Aww, Chanel." Cristal's heart ached for her pain. "He'll change his mind."

"No, he won't!" Chanel sniffed. "He's hated me for a long time, Cris. And this time...this time, I think he's found somebody else...somebody he loves...somebody from his past."

"Chanel," Cristal said gently, "it'll be all right."

"No, it won't!" Chanel flailed. "He hates me because I blackmailed him with our babies." She let out a hoarse chuckle. "But after the twins, I had to have a hysterectomy—no more babies. So how can I stop him from leaving me, now?"

"Aww, Chanel, I'm so—"

"Don't be sorry for me!" Chanel lifted her chin to fight back the tears. "Be sorry for yourself!" She sniffed. "Think of all the years you've been so envious of my *perfect* family." Chanel raised her hand to silence Cristal. "My four children represent every time my husband tried to leave me. How do you think that makes me feel?"

"But Chanel you still have your family's love—me, Mother, your kids—"

"The only reason Mother pretends to love my children was to convince Denver to stay with me." Chanel admitted hotly.

"Mother knew?"

"Of course, she knew." Chanel blistered."

"And you helped Mother dog me out so you could hold onto your man?" Cristal flared.

"Seemed like a fair trade at the time." Chanel snickered. "Besides, who else did I have to tell my troubles to?"

"But—"

Chanel sneered at the anguish in Cristal's eyes. "And all this time you thought Mother loved me best because I gave her grandchildren. Ha! Ha! Ha!" Chanel laughed wildly.

"No!" Cristal fired back. "She's always loved you best, even before your babies."

"I won't argue the point." Chanel's anger spiked. "But Mother makes a show of loving me and my children to ridicule you." Intense hatred blazed in her eyes. "And you let her."

"What?" Cristal crumbled into a nearby chair before her legs gave way; the truth slamming her like a kick in the solar plexus.

"I don't know why Mother hates you so, Cristal." Chanel took raw pleasure in turning the screws, a tactic she'd learned at her mother's knee. "But maybe it's because Daddy loved you so. But hear this—Daddy only loved you best, because for whatever reason, Mother did not." Chanel was glaring wildly. "And make no mistake, my having children—and you not—was just another way for Mother to crush you under her feet, now that Daddy's not here to protect you—"

"Stop it!" Cristal pleaded.

But there was no stopping Chanel, now. She was on a roll, and all of their little dirty secrets were fair game. "Truth be told." Chanel pushed hot words through clenched teeth. "Mother never loved me either. Her so-called love for me was just an excuse for withholding love from Daddy."

"But why Daddy?" Cristal gasped, hardly able to breathe. Her father's love had been her only constant. "All Daddy ever did…his whole life…was take care of Mother…and us?"

"Who'll ever know what makes Chantilly Moore tick? Ha! Ha! Ha!" Chanel burst into a fit of frightful laughter. "Meanwhile back in Metropolis," she wailed in her best super-hero voice, "you've been fighting the hopeless battle to win your Mother's villainous love. Ha! Ha! Ha!" She jeered. "So who's been held hostage all these years, Cristal—you or me? Or has it been both of us?" Chanel's wild laughter dissolved into pitiful, gut-wrenching sobs.

CHAPTER 23
Jasmine

Clara Clay caught the tail-end of the conversation that Beatrice was having with Jasmine in the back of the room after Bible Study—the very first one of the New Year. She was drawn to the two women when she saw the total look of devastation that Jasmine was trying to conceal under a plastered-on smile. She got there in time to hear Beatrice's closing digs and to witness the crushed expression she left on Jasmine's face.

"Sorry you couldn't make it to the New Year's Eve Ball, Jasmine." Beatrice crowed. "It was absolutely fab! But Dex gave your regrets; said you were ill."

"Y-e-s." Jasmine squeaked.

"But I thought it was kind of cute that he and his assistant...I think Dex called her...Nicole." Beatrice giggled. "I think it was absolutely inspiring that they wore matching Batman and Robin costumes." She noted the pain on Jasmine's face and cherished the moment. "I'm surprised yours would fit her, since she's so tiny and cute and all." She clucked on. "But maybe they had enough time to make it happen when Dex found out you weren't going, huh?"

"Sure." Jasmine nodded. She felt so broken she could barely stand.

"But I'm sure you'd be interested to know." Beatrice carried on with her gleeful monologue. "The two of them made quite the dynamic duo. They were the talk of the Ball." Her face twitched with wicked satisfaction. "Ta-ta! I'm off to be with my soulmate." She swept out of the room with a flourish, leaving Jasmine standing there with her heart in her hands, and her self-respect plowed under her feet.

Clara stepped toward Jasmine, maintaining her distance until she'd given her a moment to gather herself. "Hi, Jasmine." Clara's bad eye twitched. "Got a minute to help a sistah out?"

"Sure." Jasmine revived. "As long as it's you, Sis. Clara."

"Well, the custodian had to leave early, and he asked me to lock up." Clara explained. "Just want to check out the rooms before I do. Walk with me?"

"Sure." Jasmine said, grateful to be able to think about anything but her present condition.

"I saw you and Beatrice talking." Clara edged in.

"Yes." Jasmine's spirits sank desperately. "She was telling me about all the fun she had over the holidays."

"Trying to stick it to you is more like it." Clara flared in her stern church mother voice.

"Oh, she doesn't mean any harm—"

"Oh, yes, she does!" Clara whirled on Jasmine and absorbed her in a look. "And it's about time you faced up to it, too."

"Up to what?"

"Facts." Clara stated flatly.

"Facts?" Jasmine bristled. "What facts?"

"The facts about folks like Beatrice Garner—" Clara stalled, but she'd gone too far to turn around. "And the facts about your broken marriage."

"Broken marriage?" Jasmine said defensively. She wanted to dispute her, put up a fuss, but she was without the strength to do it. "What do you know about my marriage?" She sagged.

"I see you walking 'round here, putting up with things you don't believe in," Clara said bluntly. "But I tell you, Jasmine, it's no good."

"Clara, this is none of your concern—"

"I know I'm outta place." Clara's eyes bobbled. "But I'm only telling you this 'cause I care about you, Sis. Jasmine, and I can't stand to see you looking so unhappy."

Jasmine collapsed into a chair in the meeting room, no longer able to hold up her pretenses. They were far too heavy. "Oh, Clara!" She cried. "I'm so confused."

Clara sat in the seat beside her. "It'll be alright, Jasmine." She soothed. "Really, it will."

"But how, Clara?" Jasmine's hot tears began to flow. "What can I do?"

"You've gotta be honest with yourself, Jasmine. You've gotta get out in front of this thing and stare it straight in the eye...everything out in the open." Clara nodded. "Hidden motives...can kill us."

"But you don't understand, Clara!" Jasmine blubbered. "Dex promised me he'd always be true. He promised we'd always be together."

"And he mighta meant it when he said it." Clara shrugged. "Probably did. But a promise is only as good as the person that makes it. And only God is able to keep all His promises."

"But—"

"Remember our Bible Study lesson about Sarah *trusting* God and calling her husband *little* lord?"

"Sure."

"Well, I think maybe in your zeal, Sis. Jasmine, you got the whole thing a little backwards."

"What do you mean?"

"I think you've been trying to trust your husband...and make God *little* lord. Instead of trusting God...and making your husband *little* lord."

"I don't get it." Jasmine sniffed.

"We are to reverence our husbands and to serve our husbands, surely, but we can't give 'em our hearts and our souls." Clara reasoned. "Our lives belong to the one who bought and paid for 'em—Jesus Christ."

"I know that, Clara." Jasmine carped. "That's why I've tried so hard to do everything right…but I still failed God."

Clara steadied herself and fixed her gaze. "I beg to differ, Jasmine," she said.

"Why?"

"I've been watching you; slinking around here, looking all sad and sanctimonious, acting like you a martyr or something." Clara scrunched up her face. "But I think it all boils down to…pride."

"Pride?" Jasmine gasped.

"Yes, ma'am." Clara nodded. "I think it's not so much you think you failed God…as you think God failed you."

"I never said—"

"No, you'd never say it." Clara agreed. "But somewhere deep inside, you think God let you down 'cause you've been *so* right and *so* good; and God didn't give you the results you deserve."

"But I—"

"Well, you can just let all that go, Sis. Jasmine." Clara held up her hand against her friend's protest. "None o' us been so good that only good should come back around." Clara leveled Jasmine with her one good eye. "Besides, we don't do the right thing so good can come to us. We do the right thing 'cause we love the Lord, and we want to walk in His way. Ain't that right?"

"Right." Jasmine sighed.

Clara sized her up again. "So then, this po-pitiful-me act you're putting on is just pride…all dressed up in self-pity and false humility…'cause you don't want to deal with the truth."

"What truth?" Jasmine gasped.

"You've been feeling sorry for yourself, and you've been putting yourself down—"

"But—"

"No buts!" Clara held up one finger. "First, you're acting all pitiful 'cause you think you got less outta your marriage than you put in it." She held up two fingers. "Second, you're putting yourself down 'cause you didn't have the power to hold your marriage together by your own will—no matter what God's will might be for you."

"You just don't understand, Clara." Jasmine shuddered. "I've tried so hard to do everything right—"

"Sure you did." Clara softened. "But we never have the right to think what we do obligates God to do what we want. Shucks, half the time we don't even know what we want, let alone what we need."

"But don't you see?" Jasmine cried. "If I don't keep my marriage together, I'll break my vows…and I will let God down—"

"We can't let God down!" Clara's bad eye twitched. "He's holding us up! He made everything. He knows everything. And He's already forgiven us everything. Have you forgotten that, Jasmine?"

"No." Jasmine stammered badly. "But I turned myself inside out trying to keep the peace—trying to make Dex happy—so this would never happen—"

"And you thought by squeezing yourself up like that you could hold back trouble?" Clara bobbed her head. "Well, Sis. Jasmine, we ain't got the power to hold back trouble. And making less of yourself won't make nobody love you more. And letting folk treat you bad won't make nothing better." She huffed. "But there are some things we've gotta go through in this life, and that's just the way it is."

"Then why didn't God hold my marriage together?" Jasmine flinched, indicted by her own words. Putting a voice to her hidden complaint shook her to the core. But there it was, now, out in the open. "He has the power." Her words dribbled. "He knows how hard I tried to do it His way." Jasmine whimpered. "And, oh, Clara…about the pain…so much pain—"

"Awww, Jasmine." Clara folded her arms across her heavy chest to quiet the heartache she felt for her friend. "God's too big for us to pin Him down like that. He don't let us in on *why* we go through what we go through in this life, but He does give us the grace to deal with it," she said. "Things may not come out the way we think they should, but the Lord is always right there helping us handle what is."

"But Clara, why me—"

"I don't know why, Jasmine," Clara said, straining to refocus her own injured eyes. "But this I know for sure—God did not let you down; and He'll be right here with you while you're going through." She nodded. "Our part in it is to keep the faith—we gotta trust Him and love Him—no matter what."

"But Clara, I—"

"Besides, Jasmine." Clara winked with her good eye. "How else you gonna live in the seventh day?"

"What?"

"You remember, don't you?" Clara answered her own question. "God made the world and all there is in it in six days, and then He rested from all his labors on the seventh day…'cause He was finished with His work. And He wants us to follow His lead—"

"And just how do we do that?" Jasmine bristled.

"When we believe with all our heart that Jesus has already fought and won every battle for us—and finished *all* the work for us—then we can rest from our own works, just like God did from His." Clara's good eye twinkled. "And we can live in the seventh day."

"But I've tried so hard to please God—"

"But don't you see, Jasmine, our works won't cut it!" Clara reasoned. "We can't please God on our own. God is only pleased with His Son. And when we accept Jesus Christ, we are in Jesus Christ. His victory is our victory. And God is pleased with us 'cause we're in His Son—"

"What?" Jasmine's eyes widened as though she were seeing the truth for the first time.

Clara's good eye clamped down on her, and she chose her words carefully. "And when we stop trying to make things happen…and trust Jesus for whatever He allows to happen—"

"Then we can rest from all our works, too…like God did on the seventh day?" Jasmine whispered her understanding.

"Yup." Clara slumped in her chair. "We can quit striving; trust the Lord; and whatever happens…happens."

"But Clara." Jasmine blubbered. "I thought me and Dex were soulmates…like Beatrice and Harold.

"Huh?" A grin crawled across Clara's lips. "So that's it, huh? You think it didn't come out as good for you as it did for Beatrice? Ha!" She giggled. "Have I got news for you—"

"What?"

"First of all, Beatrice Garner is a liar." Clara's bad eye flinched. "And second of all, things ain't always what they seem."

"Beatrice—a liar?" Jasmine frowned. "Lying about what?"

"Girl, you running 'round here thinking Beatrice is all-that, when in fact her husband, Harold, can't stand the sight of her."

"But Beatrice said—"

"She just be putting up a front, Jasmine; more so to put you in your place than anything." Clara sat back with a satisfied grin. "She gotta be Queen Bee, which means she gotta break yo face to keep you in check. But from what I hear, Beatrice and her husband have an 'in-house' divorce."

"But they went to the New Year's Eve Ball together."

"Sure." Clara nodded. "Harold's willing to put on a big outside-show when it suits him; when there's money on the table to be had;

when being married pumps up his big-shot image." Clara chuckled. "They may reside in that big ole house together, but they don't *live* together. The lady that works for 'em is my sister-in-law's second cousin, and she tells me he lives on one side of the kitchen and she lives on the other. If they happen to bump into each other, it's when they're reaching for the same coffee pot."

"So she's just been play-acting...this soulmate stuff?"

"Yep, and she ain't the only one, Jasmine. You gotta watch them folk what always be bringing you a tale; they be making it up as they go." Clara's eyes bobbled. "The fact they be bringing it says there's more to it than meets the eye. That's why we can't put our trust in nobody but Jesus."

"But it's no better at my house, Clara." Jasmine admitted. "It nearly broke me to pieces when Dex moved out to the guest room." Her acid tears began to flow—the kind that made her eyes ache in their sockets. "I want a husband, not a roommate—"

"Not your fault—"

"But he doesn't hold me, Clara—"

"Not your fault—"

"He doesn't want me, Clara—"

"Not your fault—"

"Dex doesn't love me, Clara—"

"Don't blame yourself—"

"Oh, but I do!" Jasmine's tears overwhelmed her. "I feel like I've put my whole life into this marriage—only to find out I'm in it all alone."

"Here, again, Jasmine." Clara shook her head. "We've got to pay real close attention to the scriptures; and not listen to that mess Beatrice and them like her be spouting." She huffed. "Marriage is about submission, surely...but it ain't about submergence."

"Huh?" Jasmine sniffed.

"Jesus didn't die and rise again for you to lose yourself in some institution—whether it's your marriage, your family, your church, or your job." Clara pressed her point. "No, ma'am. He did it for *you* to be complete and whole in Him in whatever situation you find yourself. Jesus wants us to honor our husbands, surely, but not to fold our lives into their lives; because our minds, our hearts, our souls belong to Him. Remember?"

"So why do I feel so…worthless…so invisible?" Jasmine croaked.

Clara shrugged. "Maybe 'cause you've been waiting on Dex to make you feel whole, accepted, loved and—"

"And when he didn't, I started to feel like…I didn't matter."

Clara's eyes crossed. "We can walk alongside our husbands, surely, but each of us has to walk in our own lane. And our lane is set out by God and nobody else."

"Now, I see." Jasmine's voice trailed as her life ballooned into sharper focus. "The way I let Dex treat me made me hate my own self, Clara." Her tears flowed like streams. "He treated me like…I was nothing…I was a tool for his use…and I let him."

"It's okay." Clara treaded lightly.

"I let how Dex feels about me…mean more than what God says about me."

"It's okay," Clara said quietly.

"Oh, Clara, I drank in so much of his poison, I feel dead inside." Jasmine crumbled into a ball. "I'm so messed up." She sobbed. "What can I do?"

"Just let it all go, Jasmine." Clara soothed her back as she cried. "And however it come out; it come out. You can lean and depend on Jesus, now. He loves you—"

"But Dex—"

"Dex don't matter—"

"I matter." Jasmine's back straightened. The Spirit surged through her like a lightning bolt, restoring her broken posture. All the walls of her secret places came tumbling down. "Jesus loves *me*...Jasmine Davis," she whispered. "And with or without Dex...*I* matter."

"My Lord, I think she's got it." Clara cried.

The two women hugged like sisters, smiling through their veil of tears.

CHAPTER 24
Leeza

"Is this, Miss Manchester—Miss Leeza Manchester?" the man's voice said over the phone.

"It is." Leeza clipped. "Who is this?"

"I'm Detective Visclosky of the New York Police Department." He stated flatly. "And I need a minute of your time."

"The police?" Leeza questioned. "Why are you calling me?"

"This is quite a…delicate matter, Miss," the detective said. "Perhaps it would be better if you'd come down to the station."

"Down to the station?" Leeza blared. "I don't have time to come down to any station. I'm on my way to the airport. So if you have something to say, say it now or else—"

"Calm down, Miss Manchester." The detective cautioned. "I'll state my business, but I assure you at some point I will require you to come down to headquarters to sign some release papers."

"Okay." Leeza breathed. "Go ahead."

"Miss Manchester, it appears that a very unfortunate mix-up has occurred." Detective Visclosky began.

"Mix-up?" Leeza flinched. Her nerves were already humming from the stress of her latest assignment. "What sort of mix-up?"

"That's what I'm trying to tell you, Miss Manchester, if you will just listen—"

"Sorry." Leeza stilled herself. "I'm listening."

"Over the long Christmas holiday, the coroner received an exhumation order for Plot No. 229564." The detective recounted. "It was related to an ongoing murder investigation in District Court."

"Okay." Leeza snarled.

"Well, Miss Manchester, it seems that in their haste to get home to their holiday festivities, the contractor mistakenly exhumed the body from Plot No. 225964 instead." Detective Visclosky explained. "And being none the wiser, the Chief Medical Examiner performed a follow-up autopsy on that body—"

"But what does that have to do with me?" Leeza quizzed.

"Well, you see, Miss Manchester. Plot No. 225964 belongs to your mother... Mrs. Eliza Manchester—"

"What!" Leeza nearly dropped her phone. "Are you telling me you exhumed my Mom's body...without our permission...for absolutely no good reason?"

"That's what I'm telling you, Miss Manchester." Detective Visclosky floundered. "I am...the department is...very sorry for the inconvenience, but it was just an unfortunate mix-up."

"Unfortunate mix-up!" Leeza was near hysterics. "You've disturbed my Mother's final resting place, and you call it an unfortunate mix-up. This is absurd!"

"It can be disturbing, Miss Manchester. I grant you that." The detective flattened. "But it's nothing we can't fix. We'll—"

"But what you're telling me is you not only dug up my Mom's gravesite, but you also performed an unauthorized autopsy on her remains!"

"Yes, I know how this must sound, Miss Manchester," the detective said compassionately. "But according to the coroner, a prior autopsy had never been performed—"

"Of course not, you idiots!" Leeza yelled. "My Mother died in a plane crash, so there was no need for an autopsy. They already knew her cause of death!"

"Calm down, Miss Manchester." The detective warned. "This is police business, and we will make it right. But what I need to know from you is do you, or your father, want to be present when the body is reinterred?"

"No!" Leeza screamed so loud her taxi driver braked in the middle of Columbus Square. "My Dad is ill." Leeza managed.

"Chronically and severely ill." She continued. "There is no way he can come to my Mom's graveside and watch you try to fix your mistake!"

"Then what about you, Miss Manchester." The detective continued unfazed. "Would you like to be there? We can try to schedule it at a time convenient for you."

Leeza pushed out her words through clinched jaws. "What difference could it possibly make if I am there when you re-bury my Mother?" She seethed. "My Mother is dead, Detective, and this stupid blunder is yours to fix...alone."

"Then can you tell me, Miss Manchester, why is it your mother was buried in a Manhattan cemetery?" Detective Visclosky looked down at his report. "Our records show your mother was domiciled in Pennsylvania."

"My Mom wanted to be buried near her mother in the Old Church Cemetery. My Grandmother had already made the arrangements." Leeza steamed. "Is that all right with you, Detective?"

"Thank you, Miss Manchester." The detective maintained his plaintive tone and rechecked his notes. "Should we inform your father—Mr. Lee Manchester—of the situation?"

"Don't you dare!" Leeza shouted. "My Dad is ill. I will handle my Dad."

"Very well, then." The detective made a note to the file. "If we have any additional questions, I will contact you directly as next of kin. Goodbye, Miss Manchester."

"Goodbye!" Leeza clicked off the line. It was at times like these she wished she could slam down the receiver on an old-fashioned rotary phone.

Just at that moment, her phone rang again. "Hello!" Leeza shouted.

"Leeza—Gurrl—what's the matter?"

"Who is this?" Leeza growled, ready to disconnect.

"It's me…Cristal…Cristal Richardson. Remember me?

Leeza hesitated. "Atlanta airport? Hurricane Allee?"

"What was it?" Cristal teased. "My unforgettable accent or my pleasing southern personality what gave me away?"

"Sorry, Cristal." Leeza nearly gagged on her anguish. "Can't talk right now. Must go see my Dad—"

"Okay, Sweetie." Cristal's brows spiked. "Be praying for ya. Bye-Bye.

***

Immediately, Leeza cancelled her pressing flight to Sydney, Australia and beat a hasty path to have lunch with her dad in Chestnut Hill.

"What do you mean?" Lee Manchester bellowed on a single breath. "They dug up your mother's body!" His hands flailed; his eyes bulged. He readjusted his oxygen mask to take in more air. "They had no right! No right!"

"Calm down, Dad." Leeza pulled one of his kitchen chairs closer to the wheelchair he needed for the day. She spoke quietly. "You're overreacting, Dad. The police say they'll fix it—"

"They can't un-ring the bell!" Lee gurgled. "Don't they know that's hallowed ground? Don't they know?"

"Yes, Dad. They know," Leeza said evenly, trying to maintain her composure for his sake. "And they're very sorry for the mix-up—"

"Sorry!" Lee boomed. "I guess they are sorry." He panted. "Well, they'd better not touch her corpse—in any way. Leeza, you see to it! They are to return her to her resting place—and nothing more." Lee coughed. "Do you hear me?"

"Yes, Dad," Leeza said quietly. "I hear you." Seeing the state of his upset, Leeza didn't have the heart to tell him they'd already performed an unauthorized autopsy. She was afraid for his health, and rehashing the terrible error couldn't do either of them any good.

"We had finally put it all behind us." Lee protested. "And, now, they go and dig up the whole mess...all over again."

"We'll never get over losing Mom." Leeza rebutted. "But the police will fix their mistake."

"When you came all this way on any day but Sunday, I knew it had to be bad news." Lee's arms flopped onto the arms of his wheelchair.

"I wanted you to know, Dad," Leeza said reassuringly. "But I didn't want you to worry. I'll see to it that everything is done right. I promise."

"You see to it, Leeza." Lee wheezed. "You see to it, Sweet-Girl."

"I will, Dad, right away." Leeza prepared to leave for the airport to reschedule her flight. "I left you some lunch in the fridge. You just rest easy, now, and remember your heart."

CHAPTER 25
Cristal

"Thanks for agreeing to see me today, Uncle Travis," Malik said as he settled down in the cushy leather guest chair in front of Attorney Travis Johnson's impressive desk. His law offices, on Peachtree Street just south of downtown Atlanta, gave off a rich aura of great legal minds at work.

"My pleasure," Travis Johnson said. "And how's the New Year treating you?"

"All right, I guess, Uncle Travis," Malik mumbled. Although Travis Johnson wasn't blood, Malik had gotten into the habit of referring to him in family terms, as had Cristal.

"How's Cristal?" Travis strained his ear.

"As well as can be expected after that Christmas catastrophe at her mother's house." Malik groused.

"Uh-huh." Uncle Travis shook his head. "We can't associate what happened over there with Christmas," he said. "Chantilly has a way of stealing the joy out of any occasion. The way she treated Cristal and her guests from South Georgia was downright inexcusable."

"You can say that again." Malik's thick neck tensed. "And to tell you the truth, I'm getting sick and tired of it. It's not fair to Cristal, and it's not fair to me."

"I hear you." Travis sighed. "That's why I took my ball and went home."

"And that's why I wanted to talk to you, Uncle Travis." Malik continued. "'Cause you understand…and I'm at the end of my rope."

Travis locked eyes on Malik's chilly stare. "What's troubling you exactly?" he asked.

"It's not just Chantilly and her mess." Malik's voice thundered. "It's Cristal, too."

"What?" Travis leaned into his desk.

"You know we've been trying to have a baby," Malik said.

"Yes, I know." Travis confirmed. "Cristal and I talk."

"Well, it's not an easy thing for us." Malik shifted. "We've had some tests and tried some things, but nothing has worked…not yet."

"These things take time—"

"Time." Malik repeated. "That's what I keep telling Cris, but she's not hearing me. I've even taken her to counseling with our Pastor, but she—"

"She's determined?"

"Yes." Malik looked relieved at being supplied the right word. "She is determined. It's like she's trying to fight against God to have her own way, and it's making her crazy."

Travis' lips curled into a faint smile. "I've known Cristal since she was born," he said. "And she's always had tunnel vision when there's something she wants, even as a little girl."

"I know." Malik's full lips leaked out a little smile. "It's one of the things I truly love about her," he said. "But Uncle Travis, this thing with having a baby is over the top."

"I hear you—"

"And Chantilly's not helping!" Malik blasted.

"What do you mean?"

"It's like the harder Cris tries to have a baby, the more Chantilly pokes fun at her." Malik moaned. "That woman sticks it to Cris every chance she gets."

"Chantilly Moore is a very complex…and troubled woman in her own right."

"I know that." Malik agreed. "But she's getting worse, not better, especially where Cris is concerned."

"I see."

"And you wanna hear the craziest part of all?" Malik clenched his fists.

"What's that?" Travis' brow furrowed.

"I believe...I think Cristal is trying to have a baby to earn Chantilly's love and to compete with her sister." Malik blew.

Travis leaned back to consider the possibility. "Well," he said, "Chanel does have four babies; and she and Chantilly have always been...close—"

"And as crazy as it sounds, I think that's what's up." Malik pounded his fist into his hand. "Cristal feels locked out, and she wants in. But trying to kiss-up to her mama is absolutely no reason for us to have a baby."

"Agreed." Travis nodded. "Pleasing Chantilly can be a tricky proposition at best, since one rarely knows where she truly stands. I don't even think she knows...and I'm speaking from experience." Travis added. "So what're you going to do?"

Malik's jaw flexed. "I know you love Cristal," he said. "I see it in your eyes when you look at her. And I know she loves you. You're her Uncle Travis—her godfather —and her eyes sparkle every time she mentions your name." Malik sighed. "I was hoping you could talk some sense into her."

"Me?" Travis puzzled. "Do you think she'd pay any attention to what I have to say?"

"You were buds with her dad and Chantilly back-in-the-day." Malik reasoned. "You know how they rolled. You know what's up with Chantilly. You can give Cris some background, some history, anything—"

"Malik." Travis stopped him. "Is it troubling you that much, Son?"

"You bet!" Malik's voice spiked. "I love Cristal, and I really want us to have a baby. But how can we get pregnant if she stays upset all the time?" He rubbed his hands together. "And every time

142

Cris can't sleep or can't eat, because of some wild thing her mom says or does to her, I want to march right over there and grab that evil witch by her neck and choke her 'til—"

"All right. All right, Malik." Travis raised both hands. "I get the picture. It's more serious than I thought."

"Yes, it's serious." Malik steamed. "And it's getting worse by the day. You only caught a glimpse of it at that whacked-out holiday fiasco. But it needs to stop…and it needs to stop, now…or else—"

"Or else?" Travis raised his brows at the stone-cold look in Malik's eyes.

Malik chose his words carefully. "All Cris thinks about is having this baby. All Chantilly thinks about is how to gut Cris. So where's my place in all this madness, Uncle Travis? Cris treats me like I'm an after-thought." His head drooped. "And if it doesn't get better— and soon—I'll have no choice but to pull up—"

"Whoa, Malik!" Travis swung around his desk and propped on the corner nearest him. "Don't make any rash decisions you'll regret."

Malik jumped up from his chair. "Then help me make some better ones," he said, 'cause I can't go on like this—"

"I'll see what I can do." Travis agreed. "Maybe I can take Cristal to lunch—"

"You do what you do." Malik stormed out of the door. "But I can't wait forever."

CHAPTER 26
Jasmine

"Leeza Manchester!" She shrilled over her phone in the backseat of the speeding Yellow Cab. Winter was giving way to spring in Manhattan. The snow was turning to slush, and the cab driver appeared to be sloshing through every muddy puddle.

"Hi, Leeza. It's Jasmine—"

"Who?" Leeza yelled over the street noise.

"Jasmine Davis." She trilled. "Cristal Richardson asked me to give you a call."

"Oh?" Leeza paused. "Jasmine? Atlanta airport? Hurricane Allee, right?"

"Yes."

"But why're you calling me?"

"Cristal called me," Jasmine repeated, "and asked me to give you a call...to see if I can help."

"Help? Me? How?" Leeza fired.

"I don't know how, Leeza." Jasmine's voice warmed. "Cristal was just concerned. She said you sounded real upset."

Leeza breathed heavily. "To tell the truth, Jasmine, I am upset."

"Why?"

Leeza paused long enough to realize she had nothing to lose. "I'm on my way to One Police Plaza right now to meet with a detective."

"A detective?"

"Yes." Leeza hesitated. "A police matter."

"What happened?" Jasmine said consolingly.

"Long story...but it has to do with the police accidentally exhuming my Mom's body—"

"Oh, Leeza, that's awful." Jasmine soothed.

"It is awful…and very upsetting to my Dad," Leeza mumbled. "He's not well, you know."

"No. I didn't know." Jasmine sympathized. "But I'm sure this can't help matters."

"He's been so upset, and I don't understand why." Leeza groused. "No matter how many times I sit with him and explain they'll put Mom's body back where they found it, he's still frantic. But—" Leeza blew.

"But—" Jasmine encouraged her to continue.

"But I guess it doesn't help that I'm flying all over the world chasing down new clients for my boss." Leeza flustered. "In fact, after I meet with the police detective, I'm off to London today to meet with another prospective client."

"Oh, Leeza," Jasmine said sweetly. "No wonder Cristal was so concerned about you. You sound absolutely frazzled."

"I'm doing my best to keep it together." Leeza flapped. "I've been painting…a lot."

"That's good. I'm sure doing what you love helps, too." Jasmine agreed. "But at times like these, we really need the Lord."

"What?"

"Interestingly enough, that's exactly what Cristal said when she asked me to give you a call." Jasmine chuckled.

"What?" Leeza braced herself for one of Cristal's crazy comments.

"Cristal said, 'Sound to me like yo Girl need Jesus; but right now, I ain't the one to tell her…uggh!'" Jasmine giggled as she gave her best Cristal Richardson impression. "'So you call her, Jasmine, and you better make it snappy!'"

Leeza had to chuckle, too, and it felt good. "I'm sure Cristal means well," she said.

"Yes, she does." Jasmine breathed. "But it's interesting she'd ask me to call you…when my own world is falling apart."

"Falling apart?"

"Yes." Jasmine sighed. "I've been trying to hold my family together my whole life…and it's all falling apart—"

"And I've been trying to please my Dad…my boss…and, now, this whole big mess with the police." Leeza grumbled. "If it weren't for my painting…I think I'd go mad!"

"I can tell you what helped me, Leeza," Jasmine said.

"What?"

"I took my problems to Jesus, and it's made all the difference." Jasmine confided. "I feel like the weight of the whole world has been lifted off my shoulders. Because I know for myself, He's got this—"

"Yes, that might work for you." Leeza rebutted. "But remember, I'm not the religious type, and there's no need for me to start faking it now."

"I'm not asking you to fake it, Leeza." Jasmine's voice smiled. "And Jesus is not asking you to be religious—"

"Then what are you asking?" Leeza blared.

"I'm asking you to take a deep breath…and tell Jesus all about it."

"How?"

"Pray."

"But why?"

"Jesus is God, Leeza. He went to the cross for you and died for all your sins, and then He rose again with all power to keep you safe in Him." Jasmine soothed. "And, now, He wants to have a relationship with you. He wants to help you in your everyday life—no matter what you're going through."

"But even if that's true, why would He help me?" Leeza said. "I've done nothing for Him."

"Everybody you know, Leeza, wants something from you, but Jesus wants to give something to you," Jasmine said quietly. "And it's not on you; it's on Him. His love is unconditional, and He has a plan for your life."

"A plan?"

"Yes," Jasmine said. "And no matter what's going on around you; no matter who wants what from you; you can put your trust in what Jesus has done for you…and live in the seventh day."

"What?"

"I'll tell you about that later." Jasmine's voice winked. "But for right now, Leeza, just believe—believe that God is in charge, and that you matter to Him—no matter what."

"But I don't know—" Leeza stammered. "I just don't—"

"Then I'll pray for you, Leeza, like I'm praying for my own soul. And I'm sure everything'll be alright."

"You'd do that for me?" Leeza quieted.

"Yes." Jasmine pledged. "Because I'm learning we can't rely on people, or jobs, or family…not even marriage. We can't even trust our own mixed-up motives. But we can lean and depend on Jesus—"

"Gotta go!" Leeza interrupted. "I'm at the police station."

"I know you're busy, Leeza, but do take care—"

"Thanks, Jasmine." Leeza hurried as she paid her cabbie. "I know Cristal can be a bit bonkers at times…but it sure feels good knowing she cares. Will you tell her that for me?"

"Oh, no." Jasmine kidded. "You need to call her yourself."

"Okay. I will." Leeza smiled. "Bye."

CHAPTER 27
Leeza

"Miss Manchester?" Detective Visclosky scowled.

"Yes." Leeza stepped into his cramped office with a mountain-sized chip on her shoulder. It was mid-February—over a month since he'd called her about their 'mix-up'—and her deadline with Mr. Cole was looming large. The faded yellow walls and the door that looked like it had been used for target practice didn't help matters one bit.

"Come in." The detective invited warily. "Have a seat."

The cushion on the metal armchair he offered her looked a little suspect, but she wormed herself into place. "You called." Leeza's lips drew into a straight line. "You told me to come down here, and so I'm here. But I warn you; I'm booked on an international flight in less than four hours."

"That's quite all right," the detective said politely in an accent of unknown origin. "This will not take long."

Leeza lowered her briefcase to the floor and tried to make herself comfortable. "So what is it?" She pressed. "This mix-up, as you call it, has wreaked havoc on my father's health and blown my business schedule to bits."

"Like I told you over the phone," the detective droned on, "I apologize on behalf of the department for making such an unintentional error as it relates to the exhumation of your mother's remains."

"We've been through all that." Leeza frowned. "And my Dad is literally sick with worry, but we can't change any of that now."

"No, we cannot." The detective toughened.

"So why am I here?" Leeza snipped. "Could it be you're afraid of a lawsuit, Detective?"

"No, Miss Manchester, nothing of the sort." The detective grimaced at her veiled threat. "I called you in today because we wanted you to know an additional piece of information we've uncovered...but this I needed to tell you in person."

"I'm glad you called me and not my Dad." Leeza reiterated. "This whole ordeal has almost been too much—"

"Moving on and in the interest of time," Detective Visclosky said, squelching her tirade. "As I mentioned earlier, your mother's remains were not only exhumed; they were also autopsied."

"I remember." Leeza quieted down. She needed to catch her plane.

"As you will recall, Miss Manchester, the unfortunate mix-up happened over the Christmas holidays. We were short staffed, and a number of other factors ran together to cause your mother's remains to be sent directly to the Chief Medical Examiner for autopsy."

Leeza shook her head in utter exasperation. "Well, there's nothing that can be done about that now."

"No." The detective firmed. "Nothing. But in the course of our investigation, we ran into some...irregularities."

"Irregularities?"

"As you know, since your mother was the victim of a plane crash, the cause of death was evident. No autopsy was performed."

"Yes. There were over 200 people on that plane." Leeza recalled.

"And most of them were burned beyond recognition, so the emphasis was on identification, not autopsy." The detective clarified.

"Get to the point, please." Leeza shifted. "I have a plane to catch."

"In the process of the autopsy performed on your mother, Miss Manchester, we found poison in her system," the detective said bluntly.

"Poison?" Leeza gasped. "What kind of poison?"

The detective leaned over his desk. "Arsenic poison, to be exact."

"Arsenic?" Leeza flustered. "Where would my Mom have been exposed to arsenic poison?"

"Our concern, exactly." The detective nodded. "Especially in the large quantities that were discovered in her tissue samples."

"Large quantities...I don't understand." Leeza's eyes blinked vacantly. "What quantities?"

"Miss Manchester, your mother's tissue had such a high concentration of arsenic poison that the coroner estimates she probably had less than six months to live had she not been a victim of the plane crash."

"Six months...to live!" Leeza was trembling. Detective Visclosky went to his door and signaled for a sergeant to bring her some water. She accepted the styrofoam cup between shaky fingers and sipped it. The cool liquid scalded the back of her raw throat.

"Better, Miss Manchester?"

Leeza nodded. "Y-es." But she was beyond numb.

"You see, the Chief Medical Examiner can't explain away the amount of arsenic in your mother's remains." The detective continued. "Apparently, she had been poisoned slowly, over an extended period of time. Had she been complaining of illness?" he asked.

Leeza shook her head no, but then changed her mind. "Yes." She croaked. "She had been complaining of headaches and stomach discomfort for a couple of months. She even said her hair was thinning. But she laughed it off; attributed it to job stress, 'and a travel schedule that could kill a horse.'" Leeza explained. "Those were her very words."

"Well, she nearly ingested enough arsenic to kill a human; that's for sure." Detective Visclosky stated. "The medical examiner says at the rate she was going, with a few more doses, he'd have seen her on his autopsy table sooner than later."

"Oh, my God." Leeza shivered. The cup shook in her hand.

"But even then, he says he might not have identified the cause of death, Miss Manchester, because this form of arsenic is not always detectable." The detective clarified. "Your mother's death probably would've passed itself off as a heart attack at the time."

"So how did he detect it now?" Leeza challenged, unable to accept this horrific turn of events.

"Because the test we ordered for the suspected murder victim—the one involved in the court case—was more highly sophisticated than normal. You see, we were investigating a murder dating back twenty years and so—"

"So what're you saying, Detective Visclosky." Leeza labored to wrap her mind around the implications. "How did my Mom get a hold of arsenic poison?"

"That's what we'd like to know," the detective said. "We thought maybe your father—"

"My Dad cannot hear of this." Leeza pleaded. "Not with him in the state he's in, and me off to London today."

"Don't worry, Miss Manchester. "We want to take this very slow. We don't want to make any assumptions, and we don't want to make any false moves."

"Can the investigation wait until I return—"

"I can't promise you that, Miss. We take this kind of thing very seriously. We'll keep following down leads at her place of business and the like." The detective slowed. "And I will try to hold off questioning your father until you are there with him."

"Thank you." Leeza's hand shook when she smoothed her frazzled blonde strands.

"But we will have to execute a search warrant for your father's premises as soon as you return." The detective explained.

"A search warrant?"

"It's standard procedure in these matters, Miss Manchester. Your father's residence was your mother's domicile until her death."

"Of course." Leeza understood.

"But until your return, we'll be nosing around anywhere, everywhere Mrs. Eliza Manchester could have come in contact with sufficient quantities of arsenic poison to nearly cause her death."

"Sure." Leeza agreed. "Thank you."

CHAPTER 28
Cristal

"You wanted to see me, Uncle Travis?" Cristal pushed open his door in the plush offices of Travis Johnson & Associates, Attorneys at Law. "Your secretary said to come on in," Cristal said, looking stylishly sheik in pink ankle boots, pastel leggings and a matching cropped sweater. Her flawless makeup and flowing hair completed the look. The contrast of her silky brown skin and wide gray eyes made quite a stunning combination.

"Get in here, Cristal." Travis Johnson smiled broadly. He rose from his desk, as handsome as ever in a perfectly tailored three-piece suit and an eye-catching tie. His rich, brown skin had the luster of sculptured bronze, something age didn't seem to mar. "Sit down," he said. "You look as lovely as the first day of spring. I hope this was not too much of an inconvenience."

"Nope." Cristal floated into his visitor's chair. The one she'd chosen on her visits throughout her childhood. Her father had usually sat in the other on his visits with his best friend. "Beats hanging 'round the house." She smiled. "Besides, I like your office, Uncle Travis. I have since I was a little girl." She waved her hands around the elegantly appointed room. "All these books on the walls, makes it feel like a library—quiet and safe."

"Well, I don't know about all that." Travis chuckled. "But I'm really glad it makes you feel safe." His face creased. "I hope I do, too."

"Sure you do." Cristal slowed. "What's up with the serious face, Unk? Something the matter?"

"Not really, Sweetheart." Travis pushed back his chair. "But I did call you here for a serious chat."

"Well, get on with it." Cristal shifted. "You're making me nervous."

"Okay. Here it goes." Travis smiled uneasily. "Because what I have to say to you, Cris, is probably long overdue."

"O-kay." Cristal quivered.

Travis took a cleansing breath and began. "As you know, your father made a great living for Chantilly and you two girls while he was alive."

"I know." Cristal puzzled.

"And he provided handsomely for your mother in his will."

"Figures." Cristal clucked. "I knew there was some way she was able to maintain her lavish lifestyle without ever working a day in her life."

Travis nodded. "But he also provided a trust fund for you and Chanel—"

"Oh?" Cristal sat up straighter.

"Yes, it will come to each of you at age 35." Travis disclosed.

"I never knew." Cristal gaped.

"No, Morgan didn't really want you two to know." Travis admitted. "He wanted it to be a welcomed surprise when both of you had your lives already in place."

Cristal tilted her head. "Does Mother know?" she said.

"Nope." Travis winked. "Chantilly doesn't even know. It was your father's wish that it not be disclosed at the original reading of the will."

"Sneaky." Cristal smiled. "Just like him to do something like this."

"Yes. Morgan was always looking out for you and Chanel." Travis smiled. "But he didn't want the money to color your lives or affect your decisions."

"It's still a little ways off." Cristal reflected. "Chanel won't be 35 for…three years, and me, four."

"And just last year I wouldn't have thought either of you would really need it." Travis admitted. "But given your sister's current circumstances...I see she and her children may need it sooner than later.

"I guess you're right, Uncle Travis." Cristal grimaced. "With Denver gone and Chanel in such a sorry state, I guess she and the kids will need it to get back on their feet."

Travis rustled uneasily. "I have no doubt that Denver will do right by Chanel and the kids—"

"Maybe," Cristal said. "He's a pretty good guy. But you know men. Once they've kicked out the stall, ain't no telling."

Travis gave her a wry smile. "So what are you going to do with your trust fund when you get it?"

"Dunno. It's a little ways off. But trust me; I'll give it some thought."

"This money will give you and Chanel an added level of independence...from Chantilly...something I'm sure your father wanted."

"Is that why you called me down here today, Unk?" Cristal brightened.

"No." Travis breathed deeply. "Cris, the next thing I have to tell you is important...hard...but necessary. And it's going to take some time. So before we get into it, I need you to promise me that before you jump to any conclusions, you'll hear me out."

"Sounds serious." Cristal tensed.

"Don't be afraid. Don't get angry." Travis's eyes softened. "Just listen. Please."

"Okay." Cristal sat up straighter. "I've got on my big girl drawers. Shoot."

Travis Johnson, the lawyer, the man, gathered himself and began. "Malik came by to talk to me after that disastrous Christmas...mess...at your mother's house."

"He did, did he?" Cristal bristled. "He didn't say anything to me—"

"Like I said, Cris, this is going to be hard enough without you getting upset—"

"Okay-okay." She settled back down.

"Malik came by because he's concerned about you," Travis said.

"Me?"

"Yes." Travis confirmed. "He's concerned that Chantilly's attitude toward you is making you distressed, and he's afraid it could make you ill."

"Oh." Cristal shifted uncomfortably. "I admit. I did act-out after Mother's Christmas madness when I got home with Malik. But I'm over it, now."

"Are you Cris?" Travis' voice firmed. "I'm afraid this will plague you forever...until you know the whole story—"

"The whole story?" Cristal flipped a stray hair out of her eyes.

"Yes, my dear sweet child, the whole story," Travis said. He resisted the urge to run around his desk and comfort her. Instead, he gathered up his courage and continued. "As difficult as it is for me to tell you these things," he said, "unless you know the underlying reasons why your mother treats you the way she does, you'll keep getting caught up in her drama like a buzz saw." Travis straightened his handsome tie. "And Malik is right, it has already had some negative effects on your life, and it's time for them to stop." Travis bolstered himself. "And today, I'm going to give it to you...cold turkey."

"Okay, Uncle Travis." Cristal's voice broke like a little girl's. "I'm cool. I'm calm. I'm scared...but fire away."

"Have you ever wondered why you and Chanel are only a year apart, and then no more kids?" Travis opened rapid fire. "Ever wonder why your parents had two kids back to back, then nothing?"

"Yeah." Cristal admitted. "It has crossed my mind…especially since Mother acts like she adores Chanel's kids so much."

"Your house was a cold-war zone, Cristal, and you kids were the collateral damage." Travis divulged

"Why?"

Travis' eyes trailed up to the ceiling. "It was a well-kept secret…but Chantilly had an affair."

"What?" Cristal gasped. "My prim, proper, *I-can't-do-nothing-wrong* Mother had an affair? How do you know?"

"Trust me; I know." Travis nodded. "I'm the only one who does know."

"So why didn't you tell my Daddy?" Cristal pouted. "You were his best friend."

"Because it would've destroyed Chantilly if I had exposed her secret." Travis confessed. "She's a proud woman, and she had no means of support except your dad—"

"But Daddy was your friend—"

"And it would've destroyed Morgan, too—" Travis' head drooped.

"But who?" Cristal pressed.

Travis gripped the arms of his chair. He squeezed so hard it numbed his fingers. "It would've destroyed your father," he murmured, "if he had ever suspected…it was me."

Cristal choked, hardly able to catch her breath. "You?" She shrilled.

"Yes, Cristal."

"You?" She covered her mouth with one hand, afraid of what might come next.

"I'm as ashamed of my actions today as I was back then, Cristal." Travis pinned himself to his chair. "But not of you, Baby…never of you."

"You?" Cristal shook her head violently. "You...you're my...Daddy?"

"Yes, Cristal—"

"Why didn't you tell me?" Cristal sobbed. "Why didn't somebody tell me?"

"I couldn't." Travis' voice softened. "I could only stay close enough to your family to be sure you were alright."

"You had an affair with your best friend's wife!" Cristal glowered at him. "What kind of man are you?"

"It was only that one time—that one horrible time." Travis shuddered. "Chanel was just a baby; your daddy was out of town on the railroad, and I stopped by your house to drop off some legal papers."

Cristal slammed her hand on his desktop. "And that was enough for you to cheat with your best friend's wife—"

"I'm not trying to excuse myself." Travis jammed his fist into his forehead. "I was wrong...but your mother was having a real difficult time adjusting to the baby. I later realized she was having a terrible bout of post-partum depression—"

"Uggh!" Cristal growled. "What're you saying? You took advantage of her?"

"No. But it was as much my fault as hers." Travis explained. She was in pain and I was angry...a lethal combination. I should've never stopped by without your dad being home—"

"So why did you come by when you knew my Daddy was away?" Cristal sizzled.

"My fiancée, Nancy Rawlings, was your mom's best friend at the time, and she had just dumped me that very day." He rubbed his hands together. "And I guess I went by your house to be consoled in some way by Chantilly. I thought maybe she could convince Nancy to take me back. But I never expected—"

"She'd jump your bones." Cristal said flatly, struggling to regain her equilibrium.

"And looking back on it, I guess I did it, not to hurt your dad or your mom, but I did it in a red hot rage. I wanted to hurt Nancy Rawlings like she'd hurt me." He looked up sheepishly at Cristal. "But I ended up hurting everybody I loved; especially, you."

"Go on." Cristal said coolly, scrubbing at her tears with the backs of her hands. Her makeup was a mess.

"It was just that one time." Travis continued. "I had hoped nothing would come of it. I knew it would never, ever happen again. So I pushed the incident to the back of my mind and made myself scarce until your father returned."

"And then nine months later, there I was?"

"And we were all surprised, particularly your father, who had been trying to give your mom space so she could recover."

"But he couldn't be sure?"

"No. He couldn't be sure." Travis lowered his head. "And he confided his feelings in me…his best friend."

"Did you discuss it with Mother?" Cristal said bitterly.

"No." Travis sagged limply. "By then she was treating me like nothing ever happened, and I liked it that way. It was the only way I could look your father in the eye."

"But my Father wasn't fooled." Cristal sat up like a brave child. "Not my Father."

"No." The lawyer flinched. "Over the years, he noticed how your mother treated you. At first, he thought she resented you for having two babies back-to-back."

Cristal squinted. "Two babies in diapers?"

"Yes." Travis nodded. "Plus, I think your mother lived with the hope it wasn't true. That you were her husband's child—"

"But—"

"But as you grew up, she couldn't be sure." Travis reasoned. "And she resented you for that, too."

"Aaah...so daddy showed me more love to make up the difference." Cristal reflected.

"Something like that." Travis agreed. "And as you grew into the beautiful young lady you are today, his doubts were renewed."

"Why?"

"Morgan knew something was up when out of his light-skinned family came this brown-skinned baby." Travis faced her. "And then he started to wonder why your mother always made such a point of saying that you looked like your cousins on his side of the family—the darker hued ones."

Cristal breathed hard and took a long look at Uncle Travis—her new daddy—tall, handsome, and beautifully brown. "So what did my Father do?"

"He asked me to get a DNA test done. He brought me a hair sample from your comb—"

"What?"

"I tried every trick in the book to talk him out of it." Travis flustered. "I reasoned with him that no good could come from him knowing. But he had to know—at least know. The relationship with your mother was driving him crazy—the tension, the temper, the secrets. And he was determined that no child under his roof would be destroyed by it—no matter who your biological father might be." Travis leaned forward. "Morgan genuinely loved you, Cristal. You were his sweet, little girl—"

"So you got the test?" Cristal pushed him along.

"Yes." Travis answered. "I had no choice."

"And it showed that I was not his biological daughter." She posed it more as a statement of fact than a question.

"Yes."

Cristal's face creased. "Does my Mother know?"

"No!" Travis held up both hands. "Your daddy never said a word to your mother about his suspicions…not ever."

"Why?"

"He loved Chantilly dearly—"

"So why didn't you tell her?"

Travis raised his brows. "I don't think your mother wanted to know for sure," he said. "It's as though not knowing could shield her from her shame, absolve her of her guilt…and your daddy's questioning eyes. But I believe she even started to hate your daddy because she suspected he knew and was holding it over her head."

"So you got the DNA results." Cristal reiterated.

"Yes."

"And what did my Father do?" She frowned.

"Swore me to secrecy—"

"He never thought it could be you?" Cristal clipped.

"Never." Travis' voice cracked. "He was my best friend…always my best friend. And he sat right there in that chair next to you and wrote you this note." He reached into his desk and handed her an envelope embossed with his logo.

"What does it say?" Cristal's hand shook as she received the envelope.

"You should read it for yourself," Travis said. "But he told me to give it to you only in the event the tensions between you and your mother became too great for you to handle."

Cristal eyed her Uncle Travis. "And you've held this secret…all these years—"

"You've got to know, I've loved you all these years, too, Cristal. And I've been keeping a close eye on you all these years." Travis pushed back his tears. "And when I saw the way Chantilly treated you at that Christmas brunch, it was all I could do to hold my peace. But then Malik came to see me, and I knew it was time—"

"Did you tell Malik?" Cristal shrieked.

"Oh, no!" Travis raised his hands. "No! I didn't tell him any of this—"

"But you couldn't hold the truth back from me...any longer." The hard edge softened in Cristal's eyes.

"Yes." The lawyer felt relieved, like he'd finished the longest deposition of his life. He sat still and waited.

Cristal lowered her head and sat quietly for a long while. Then she rubbed her hands together, shot him a half smile and said, "So what do I call you, now?"

"Oh," Travis said, able to breathe again. "I hope you'll continue to call me Uncle Travis. Your mother can't know any of this."

"Why not?" Cristal arched her back like a warrior. "She just oughta know."

"I know she doesn't show it." Travis' eyes pleaded. "But your mother is a fragile human being. And if she even had an inkling that you knew her secret—that you could take up where your father left off—make her feel guilty and defensive. Well, I don't know, it could destroy her."

Cristal considered his words. "So you think she has enough on her hands right now, what with Chanel to deal with; is that what you're saying?"

Travis braced himself on his desk. "Cristal, I'm asking you to be...compassionate."

"Do you know how that woman's treated me?" Cristal's eyes lowered into slits. "Held out her love like a carrot on a stick to me! Made me think I could have it if I danced to her music—talked right, looked right, acted right...gave her some grandchildren?"

"You can't tell her, Cristal." Travis entreated. "She's your mother—"

"Even knowing what I know?" Cristal pursed her lips in defiance.

162

"She named you Cristal because she paid a high price for having you." Travis reminded her. "You cost her her pride, her peace of mind, and ultimately her marriage. And I don't know if she can ever forgive you."

"Forgive me? Hah!" Cristal bellowed. "I don't know if I can ever forgive her!" She held her head to the ceiling to stave off her tears. "I tried to make my Mother love me. I drew her pictures and tried to give her butterfly kisses, but she wanted none of it. She made a game of letting me see her give all her kisses to Chanel, and not to me."

"But you can't tell her; it could kill her." Travis warned. "And if it doesn't kill her physically, it could destroy her mentally. Chanel is already acting like a pillar of salt—stuck in place. You're already raising Chanel's four kids." Travis slowed. "And I'm real proud of you and Malik for that, Cristal. But you don't want to have your mother on your hands, too; now, do you?"

"So I'm supposed to keep her nasty little secret just to keep her sane?" Cristal flexed her neck. "I can't promise you that." She blasted. "The big phony!"

"I know Chantilly has treated you rotten all your life, Cristal," Travis said. "But it has made you the stronger person."

"Me?" Cristal's head fell back as she laughed. "Strong?"

"Yes, you…strong and very much loved." Travis couldn't stop himself. He came around the desk and held his daughter in his arms. "You're my daughter, Cristal Richardson, and I'm so very proud of you. I love you…and my best friend loved you, too."

As Travis held her in his arms, Cristal gave the man she'd known all her life new consideration. She remembered all the birthday parties, and pony rides on his aching back, and praises, and gifts, and glances. She knew she could always count on Uncle Travis—her father's best friend. Cristal leaned into his arms and hugged him like she'd done so many times before. But this time, she was hugging her very own flesh and blood. She whispered, "Daddy."

CHAPTER 29
Jasmine

"Surprise!" Madeline burst into her dad's office unannounced, luggage in tow. Her Spring Break trip to Hawaii had been unavoidably cancelled. Since he'd told her he was working on the Freeman case late most nights at the office, she thought she'd give her daddy a try. Besides, she wasn't ready to face her mother yet and all of her interminable questions about her up-ended vacation plans.

"Madeline?" her dad said without turning around to face her. He was fully clothed. But the woman he had bent over his antique office desk was not. The woman swooped down to the floor, swept up her pile of clothes, and scrambled past Madeline. Her head was down, blonde hair shielding her face, and the handful of clothes attempting to hide her nakedness. But Madeline recognized the well-built young woman as Nicole Saxton, her dad's executive assistant. Nicole couldn't have been more than 10 years her senior. Madeline was motionless; time stood still. The smell of stale sweat and raw bodies was stinging in her nostrils.

"Madeline, what are you doing here?" Her dad repeated with his back to her while he dealt with the matter of his open zipper.

Madeline's mouth moved, but she couldn't speak.

"It's not what you think, Madi." Her daddy blubbered as he turned to approach her, straightening his tie and tucking in his shirt tails.

The absurdity of his words gave Madeline back her voice. "Oh, yeah." She blistered. "And what might that be, Dad. What am I thinking?"

"There's nothing between Nicole and me. Not really." He fished for words to explain. "It's just sex."

"Just sex?" Madeline struggled not to scream. "Does my Mother know about this, 'just sex'?"

"Of course not," Dex said. "Why should she?"

"Duh!" Madeline rocked her head from side to side. "Because she's your wife! Because who you have sex with, she has sex with! Because it would kill her if she knew—"

"And that's exactly why I don't want her to know." Dex squared his shoulders. "I would never hurt your mother, Madi."

"So what are you doing, Dad?" Madeline laid her eyes on him as though she were looking at him for the first time. "And don't give me that 'just sex' crap. I know you too well for that. I'm your only daughter...at least, I guess—"

"Of course, you are, Madi. You're my only baby." He came closer, but her board-stiff body warned him not to touch. "All of my professional life, Madi...white men have lorded over me in one way or another." Dex's voice took on a decidedly serious tone. He sounded as if he were about to make a summation speech before the most crucial jury of his career. "White men have made me grovel at their feet for every scrap they've tossed my way. They've determined if, when, and how successful I can be—"

"So what is this?" Madeline propped her hands on her hips. "*The white-man-made-me-do-it* defense?"

"I'm just trying to make you see what I've had to go through all these years." Dex pulled Madeline down to sit beside him on the leather couch. "I've had to take their crap to put a roof over our heads and send you to the finest schools. And while they've been screwing over me, I've had to take it with a smile." Dex wrung his hands. "To even get a shot at making partner, I've had to put in torturous hours and scrape the bottom of the barrel to find the clients they didn't want—"

"So what, Dad?" Madeline stopped him in his tracks. His pathetic excuses were making her flesh crawl. "Every lawyer on the rise has to go through—"

"Not like me!" Dex blistered. "Not like a black man, Madeline. Never like a black man."

"You're caught up in the 80's, Dad." Madeline seethed. "Everybody's not out to get you now. This is just how the business world works."

Dex grabbed Madeline by the shoulders to make her see. "Last year, they passed me over for partner for a younger guy...a white guy. I had more seniority. I had more billable hours. I had more experience and toughness. But they said he had more connections. Ha!"

"But you and Mom—"

"Your mother?" Dex defended. "I try to tell her about herself; try to get her to fix herself up," he said. "She's dumpy and plain, and all the partner's wives are skinny fashion plates. They laugh at her behind her back. But she won't hear me." He huffed. "They make a big deal about liking Jasmine's *world-famous* brownies, while they're secretly thumbing their noses at us." Dex bristled. "They tolerate us, like some throwbacks to the Jeffersons...but that's not the same as accepting me on my merit."

"So you're angry with your white bosses." Madeline shook his hands off her shoulders. "I get that. Half of America is." The couch squeaked when she shifted away from him. "But what's that got to do with—"

"But I'm not angry with their white women." Dex's voice took on a sinister tone. "Oh, no," he said. "Their women are my...prize...my revenge for all the hell they've put me through. And I mean to take down as many of them as I can—"

"Oh, I see," Madeline said viciously. "You only bend white women over your office desk in the dead of night…while my Mother is sitting at home alone?"

"That's right." Dex's chest swelled. "It's my way of sticking it to them for sticking it to me all these years." His head dribbled into his hands. "And it is just sex, Madi." He pleaded. "Your mom doesn't need to know. She'll forgive me. She has to forgive me—seventy times seven."

"You need help, Dad." Madeline said dispassionately. "And you need to tell Mom…or I will."

Dex jumped up off the sofa. "I can't tell Jazz this. I've been trying to protect her," he said. "I'll move out before I have to face her with this."

"Yeah." Madeline's arm trembled as she pointed to his antique desk where she'd seen his disgusting display. "And this is how you protect my Mother?" she said, pushing off the sofa and trudging to the open door. The short walk felt like a 100 miles of badlands. "I'll stay at a hotel tonight, Dad." The pain cracked in her voice as she retrieved her luggage. "And you have your stuff out of my Mom's house before I go home tomorrow." The door clicked softly behind her.

CHAPTER 30
Leeza

Leeza landed at Heathrow Airport and checked into the chic King George Hotel near the River Thames. Although her concern for her dad and her career threatened to overwhelm her at times as she crossed the Atlantic, Jasmine's encouraging words offered her a great deal of comfort on the eight-hour flight. Her phone call had come like a breath of fresh air before her devastating meeting with Detective Visclosky and the horrible news about her mom being slowly poisoned to death. Leeza was able to get room service and a well-deserved good night's sleep in her elegant suite overlooking the brisk English street life below. The fog had lifted. London was enjoying the promise of spring, and nothing could be lovelier.

The next evening, her two friends, Heather and Nadine, whom she'd met during her Harvard days, told her to wear something hip and sexy. "And try not to look like a stuffy, old business frau," they had giggled over the phone. Leeza picked out a little black number and a push-up bra for the occasion that put her supple cleavage and long, silky legs on full display. At midnight, her friends picked her up at her hotel, all black eyes and glitter, and took her to an underground Rave. Heather was wearing red silk shorts and a strappy tee, and Nadine had on a purple, spandex mini that barely covered her assets. Nadine had brought over her henna kit for the occasion, and she scrawled a temporary tattoo down Leeza's neck— a long, bright red butterfly.

The three of them stumbled down some steep stairs to what must have been an abandoned railroad tunnel for the Tube, the equivalent of a subway tunnel in New York City. They entered the club-like setting, colored lights strobbing and music pumping out a loud, monotonous dance track. The room was filled with odd creatures and phantom faces—green hair, spiked brows, extreme piercings—and varying states of lucidity. What was passing itself off for dancing was a lot of pushing and shoving, gyrating and banging.

The L-shaped, crystal bar was lined with young, scantily clad women of all ages, each dripping with a come-hither look in their eyes that said they were ready for anything. Leeza's two friends snagged two places at the bar and squeezed her in between them. They could barely hear each other talking over the loud music.

"So where is he?" Leeza yelled.

"Patience my dear, Leeza," Heather said in her British brogue. "This is London, not New York. The real party doesn't start 'til 3 a.m."

"He'll be here." Nadine wiggled, trying to get the attention of every man passing by.

"He is so delectable," Heather said.

"Don't worry." Nadine purred. "You're sure to spot him the minute he comes through the door."

The two friends moved to the dance floor to bounce around to the heavy metal downbeat, leaving Leeza to fend for herself at the bar. She received a number of admiring glances, from men and women alike, but she was trying to keep her mind on her business. She'd come here to meet Rhymes Nolan, the son of Lord Jeffrey Nolan, head of Sebatha Enterprises. Her friends from Harvard, Heather and Nadine, had had the good fortune of meeting him in this very spot some months back, and they had made fast friends. For old time sakes, they were prepared to let Leeza cash in on their goodwill.

"There he is." Heather mouthed and motioned to the door.

"Yes." Nadine giggled absurdly. "The finest man in the room."

After being greeted and pawed on by a gauntlet of inebriated patrons, Rhymes made his way to the bar. He didn't acknowledge Heather or Nadine until he'd slipped a nod to the bartender who seemed eager to respond to his slightest inflection. Once he had his liquor in a tall snifter, Rhymes took up the spot quickly vacated by some clubbers who obviously respected his superior clout. He assumed a nonchalant pose with his elbows turned to face the bar.

"Ladies." Rhyme finally snapped his fingers at Heather and Nadine, and they came running. "Fancy meeting you here," he said in his cultured English accent.

Heather and Nadine swooned as if on cue. They flanked him, one on either side, and stroked his arms through his tailored silk shirt. His spiked hair was an abnormal shade of blonde and the piercing in his left nostril appeared to be removable upon necessity.

"Rhymes, you naughty boy; we've been waiting for you." Heather cooed.

"And who do we have here?" Rhymes gave his first notice of Leeza. He liked the looks of her, and his eyes lapped her up like a saucer of milk.

"This is the friend we were telling you about, Rhymes." Heather said, dripping his name like honey.

"And what is your name, *Friend*." Rhymes scrolled his eyes over Leeza's sexy cleavage.

"Leeza." She stopped with that, since first names seemed to be the protocol. And after all, she didn't want to come off as a hungry, frustrated, tired businesswoman. Even though, at that moment, she was all three.

"Not drinking?" Rhymes glanced at her empty hand. He had an immediate distrust of people who didn't indulge in some form of intoxicant. After all, what was the point?

"I'll have what you're having." Leeza said seductively, trying not to appear too forward.

Rhymes nodded at the bartender, again, and in less than a second, he was placing a fancy, long-stemmed glass into her hand.

Leeza sipped and smiled like she had a secret she was dying to tell.

After Heather and Nadine had fawned over him for an appropriate amount of time, Rhymes yelled over the music in Leeza's direction. "Dance?" He nodded to the crowded floor.

"Sure." Leeza let him lead the way. "If you'll show me how."

Rhymes seemed to like the invitation, and he happily lead her out to the mob scene in the center of the floor.

"Come here often?" Leeza mouthed to get his attention, since he seemed to be x-raying all of the women within radar range.

Rhymes looked back at her as if he were seeing her for the first time. He smiled and cocked his head. "What do you want?"

"Want?" Leeza balked.

"Sure." He waved his arms over his head like the crazy mob around them. "Everyone who wants to meet me…wants something."

Leeza waved her arms around, in-kind, like she was a woman gone mad. "To be honest," she said close to his ear, "I do want something."

"Name it." Rhymes looked amused. "And we'll see what I can do."

Leeza went for it. "I need your father's business." She buzzed.

Rhymes pulled Leeza away from the dance floor so they could hear each other better. "I usually get—how does my Father put it in his antiquated terms—'serviced'—to render this sort of favor to anyone." He grinned lustfully.

Leeza thought back to her Dad's subtle suggestion that she should do whatever was required to pull this off, and she cringed. She'd never expected to be called on to lay her body on the line to keep her job. "Serviced?" she said tightly as she continued to bounce to the beat of the wicked music. "But all I'm asking is that you give me an introduction to the CEO at your father's firm."

"That's a tall order." He pulled her closer to him and grinded his body against hers. "Even for you, Pretty Leeza."

Leeza was repulsed by his touch, but she didn't dare move. She wanted to run away and yell, "Later for this job!" But she gritted her teeth and said nothing.

Rhymes twirled her away from him and then pulled her ear back to his lips. "But," he said, "I may be willing to let you off lightly." He nodded to Heather and Nadine who were salivating over him like tigers on the prowl; eyes glued to his every move. "Because I imagine your girlfriends over there," he crooned, "are more than willing to provide enough 'service' to cover this one favor—this one time. He skinned his lips back over perfect white teeth and snarled like a wolf.

Leeza kept still and prayed with all her heart that this would pass.

"Tell you what I'll do." Rhymes looked over his shoulder at Heather and Nadine, again, who were nearly panting with desire and anticipation. "I'll give your name to my Father's executive aide…with my recommendation." Rhymes ran his index finger along her cheek and down her neck over the glowing butterfly. "Will that please you?"

"Oh, yes. Thank you." Leeza dared to breathe again, but every part of her body was gripped with fear as to how far she'd have to go, if asked.

Rhymes eyes revealed that something was kicking in that was far more potent than the liquor in his glass. "And what you do with it, Pretty Leeza," he slurred, "that's entirely up to you." He gave her cheek a long, slow lick with his hot, wet tongue. "But I never want to see you here again. Understood?" He staggered slightly.

"Understood," Leeza whispered. She wanted to use her hand to scrub him off her cheek. It felt like it had been fire-branded, but she didn't dare. She slithered back over to the bar with her girlfriends and felt like the lowest form of snake.

CHAPTER 31
Cristal

When Cristal left the office of her newfound daddy—Travis Johnson—she streaked up I-85 at breakneck speeds in her red Cadillac STS. She was more concerned about having it out with her mother than she was with getting a ticket from the Atlanta Police. Travis' warnings were ringing in her ears: "Your mother's too fragile. Your mother's too sensitive." But despite his pleas, Cristal wasn't about to let Chantilly off the hook. "Well, duh, I'm sensitive, too!" She fumed, as she drove with one hand and repaired her makeup in the rearview mirror with the other.

Cristal skidded to a stop on Chantilly's white-stoned driveway, just short of plowing headlong into the steel garage doors. She jumped out of her car and marched to the front door, arms pumping at her sides like a warrior on the ready. Cristal jabbed the doorbell and patted one foot in her four-inch heels as she waited.

"Cristal?" Chantilly blurted her name like a curse word. "What are you doing here this time of day?" Her brow furrowed. "Is something wrong with one of Chanel's children?"

Cristal didn't want to blow her mission by being refused entry. So she calmly said, "Everything's fine, Mother. I just need to speak with you for a moment, please."

"Well, alright." Chantilly moved aside and allowed her entrance. "But I can't imagine—"

"Where's Chanel?" Cristal said as she moved into the kitchen with Chantilly trailing.

"Upstairs…resting." Chantilly sighed. "She had an appointment with her psychiatrist this morning, and it's taken a toll on her. He insisted she take a sedative and a long nap."

"Good," Cristal said. "I'm glad my dear sister is asleep. It'll make our discussion that much more…private." She seated herself in the breakfast nook, and Chantilly followed suit. "And what is Chanel's shrink saying these days?"

"Her doctor." Chantilly corrected. "Her doctor says Chanel is making great progress…but she's not quite ready to resume her full duties." Chantilly settled into her seat. "That reminds me, Cristal," she said. "In honor of Chanel's wonderful progress, I was thinking we should have the twins' birthday party over here next month. You can bring them over and—"

"That's not why I'm here," Cristal said flatly. "We'll have to discuss that at another time."

"Then why are you here, Cristal?" Chantilly bristled. "I don't remember inviting you—"

"You can cut the bull, Lady!" Cristal blared and slapped both hands on the table between them. She glared at her mother with red-hot orbs. "Your secret is out!"

"What?" Chantilly flustered. "Have you lost your mind coming into my home, behaving in this manner—"

"Cut it!" Cristal snarled. "You've had your last time trying to make me tuck tail and run." Her gray eyes flickered. "Now, I know you for the lying, low-down witch you are; and not the elegant lady you pretend to be."

"What?" Chantilly's jaws flapped. "If you're referring to our little Thanksgiving snafu," she said, "we simply got our wires crossed—"

"Drop it!" Cristal lowered her voice and slowed her pace. "I had a long talk today…with my Daddy."

Chantilly gasped. "How dare you, Cristal." She hissed. "Your father is dead."

"Yes." Cristal's whisper carried as much force as Hurricane Allee. "My Father—the man who loved me; the man who raised me;

the man who accepted me as his own—is dead." She hurled her words with lightening force. "But my Daddy—the man you slept with to bring me into this world—Travis Johnson—is not!"

Chantilly fell back as if her words were a hard slap to the face. "Cristal?" She stammered. "What are you saying?"

"Don't try to deny it, Woman!" Cristal's words clamped down on her like a viper. "We have the DNA test to prove it."

"But I never knew—"

"Quit lying!" Cristal nearly screamed. "For once in your miserable life, Chantilly Moore, quit lying, and face up to the truth!"

"But I never knew—"

"You didn't know because you didn't want to know." Cristal slung her words back at her. "You had all the evidence staring you right in the face every time you looked at me; but you didn't want to admit the truth to my Father—God rest his soul—to Travis, to yourself...and God forbid, to me!"

Chantilly cried. "But I never knew—"

"You knew you had sex with another man! You knew you cheated on your husband! You knew you were guilty of adultery!" Cristal tossed bombs at her in rapid fire. "You could've started there!"

Chantilly covered her ears. "Stop! Stop it, Cristal!" She cried. "Say no more!"

"You got it!" Cristal reared back in her chair and folded her arms across her curvy bosom. "I'm through talking to you." She rolled her neck like a champion boxer. "Now, it's your turn to talk to me."

Chantilly looked up to the ceiling trying to stanch her tears. "Don't you see? I couldn't tell the truth." She sniffed. "The truth would've killed your father; it would've killed his relationship with his best friend; it would've killed our marriage; it would've killed...you."

"Oh?" Cristal stared at her incredulously. "So, now, you'd have me believe you've been lying all these years to protect me? Ha!" She sneered.

Chantilly clasped her perfectly manicured hands, which were trembling fiercely. "Well, it's true. I felt guilty for what I'd done, but I'd hoped nothing would come of it; it was only that one time. And I'd hoped that things would stay as they'd always been." Chantilly faltered. "But as I watched you grow up, Cristal, looking so beautiful and so much like…Travis…and his family…I just couldn't admit to myself that one foolish night could've turned our whole world upside down."

"And for your own guilty, little sin—" Cristal raised her head to prevent her own tears. "You took your hatred out on me all these years?"

"I didn't hate you, Cristal." Chantilly's voice quivered. "I don't hate you." She tried to make sense of it herself, maybe for the first time. "I guess I just felt I had to keep up appearances. Your father was a man of prominence." She looked at the hurt in her daughter's eyes, and her pretenses shattered like crystal. "Or maybe my guilt…the whole sordid mess of what I'd done…did spill over onto you." Chantilly reached both hands across the table toward Cristal, but she did not reach back. "You're my baby, Cristal." She cried freely. "I love you…and I am so, so sorry I hurt you."

Some of the fire ebbed out of Cristal's words when she was finally able to speak. "If it hadn't been for my Father—your husband—and Malik," she whispered, "do you know I mighta…harmed myself when I was younger?" Her tears finally flowed. "I thought you hated me 'cause I wasn't good enough, pretty enough—as good as Chanel—and you made me hate myself, too."

"Oh, my poor, sweet baby." Chantilly wrung her hands. "I've caused so much damage," she whispered. "Your father was good to me, to us, and I made his life a living hell to cover up my own—"

She broke down into blubbering sobs. "I wish I could take it all back. I wish—"

"Well, you can't, Mother." Cristal sobered. "You can't take any of it back," she said. "All we can do, now, is to be honest with each other...and move forward."

"But how—" Chantilly faltered. "How can we—"

"I forgive you, Chantilly Moore." Cristal's words leaked out, one by one. "Everything you've done to me...all the pain...all the lies...all the wasted years of trying to please you...I forgive you."

"But you called me Chantilly?" Her mother gasped.

"From this day forth, that's who you are to me," Cristal said quietly. "I ain't got nothing but love for you, but I am not willing to pretend I'm nothing so you can feel like you're something—not ever again."

"Ohh!" Chantilly bowed her head in shame. "I've lost the right to be called your mother?"

Seeing her crushed spirit, Cristal rose and draped her arms about her mother's neck. "It's not that," she said tenderly. "I'm not trying to punish you. But from here on out, we've gotta build a new relationship—me, you, Daddy-Travis, Malik and Chanel. And me calling you Chantilly will remind all of us that our new relationship has to be built on the truth."

Chantilly shivered as she clung to her daughter. "Yes, Baby, you're right," she said, "on the truth."

CHAPTER 32
Jasmine

Madeline crept up the walkway alongside the fully-enclosed Olympic-sized swimming pool in the rear courtyard. She wanted to enter the house by the side entrance so she wouldn't have to encounter her mother on her first night back home after her failed Spring Break trip. She wanted to sneak up the back stairs, bury herself under the covers in her old bedroom and get a good night's sleep. She'd given it a lot of thought in her hotel bed the night before. She would tell her mother the truth about what she'd witnessed in her dad's office. But she wanted one more night's peace before dealing with her mother and her hysterics.

She'd gotten as far as the kitchen when she heard her mother call out, "Madeline? Baby? Is that you?"

Madeline took a deep breath and rounded the corner into the kitchen. "Yes, Mom." She dropped her bags. "It's me." Jasmine was seated at the breakfast nook drinking a cup of black coffee. Madeline leaned over and gave her mother a tight squeeze. "My trip got cancelled." She shrugged.

"Ahh, Baby." Jasmine sounded genuinely concerned. "I'm real glad you're home. But what happened? You were so looking forward to your first trip to Hawaii."

"I know, Mom, but the Ambassador was called away suddenly. There's some unrest in his government, and he was called home for an emergency briefing." Madeline explained. "And under the circumstances, he didn't want his family to go to Hawaii without him."

"Must be serious?" Jasmine frowned.

"Serious enough for Ambassador Acho to stash his whole family away in a safe-house somewhere in the District until he returns."

Madeline glimmered. "That's why I came on home. I didn't want to be a bother…or in the line of fire."

"Wise move." Jasmine appraised her only child with a careful eye. She was slimmer, now, and even more beautiful than when she dropped her off at Howard. "Besides, I've missed you desperately."

"Ahh, Mom." Madeline hated her mother's lavish shows of affection. "Imani begged her dad to let us go on the trip alone. She wanted to show off all her new bikinis." Madeline winked. "But the Ambassador wouldn't hear of it. He's so protective of his only daughter."

"I should say so." Jasmine's eyes widened. "I'm equally protective of mine," she said. Her daughter had grown up so much in the months they'd been apart. But she wouldn't have wanted to see these two, only daughters, traipsing off to the Big Island, alone.

"So, the trip is off until we can all go together." Madeline pursed her lips. "No biggy. It'll be fun then, too."

"Sit here with me, Madeline." Jasmine pulled her over to the grey leather sectional in the den. "I have some sad news for you, Baby." She held both of her daughter's hands gently in hers. "You see…your dad's moved out. He came by and got most of his things late last night." Jasmine tried to squeeze back the tears. "But I'm sure it's only temporary. You know, he's under a lot of stress at the office—"

"I know." Madeline shook her hands free.

"You know?" Jasmine frowned. "You know what?"

Madeline averted her eyes. "You see, Mom, I didn't get back just now." She squeaked. "Actually, I got back last night."

"You did?" Jasmine gawked. "So where—"

"I stopped by Dad's office when I got in last night." Madeline clipped.

"Was he there?" Jasmine's eyes flickered.

"Yep, he was there, alright." Madeline's face scrunched into a tight ball. "Actually…I caught him and Nicole in the office…together."

"His assistant, Nicole?" Jasmine deflected. "Oh, they often work late. You know your dad is in the throes of one of the most important cases of his career. He—"

"Quit it, Mom!" Madeline jumped up off the couch, ready to explode. She couldn't stand the lies and her mother's charades another second. No matter how it might hurt, it was time for the truth to be heard, like a light shining in darkness. "Mom, I'm not a little girl you have to protect anymore," Madeline said flatly. "I caught them together…with her dress up and his pants down. Dad and Nicole…having sex."

"Oh, no!" Jasmine shuddered. "Baby, I hate you had to see such a thing."

Madeline returned to the couch and comforted her mother. "It's okay, Mom. It was good I saw it firsthand." She rocked her softly. "You're always trying to protect me at your own expense. You've been doing that my whole life, and it hasn't helped me…or you."

"I didn't want you to know, Madeline." Jasmine wiped her tears with the throw. "But this is not the first time—"

"Oh, really?" Madeline's brows spiked.

"Baby, your dad was accused of sexual harassment last year," Jasmine said quietly, trying to soften the blow. "It killed his chance to make partner."

"Oh?" Madeline bristled at hearing the other side of his lie. "And what happened?"

"The partners paid the woman off. They thought she was lying." Jasmine faltered. "They think we're a close-knit family."

"And that's because of you, Mom." Madeline observed. "But didn't that make you suspicious?"

"Of course, it did." Jasmine admitted. "But I tried to forgive and forget. Dex promised me nothing happened, and I wanted to believe him for your sake, for our family's sake." Jasmine sniffed. "Besides, the firm has forgiven your dad that one indiscretion. They're considering him for partner, again."

"About that—" Madeline grimaced. "Dad called me before I got here. It seems that after last night's *indiscretion*, Ms. Nicole Saxton has given your husband an ultimatum."

"Ultimatum?"

"Yes, Mother." Madeline set her teeth on edge. "It seems she wants him to leave you and marry her…or else—"

"Or else, what?" Jasmine's chin dropped.

"Or else…she'll accuse Dad of sexual harassment…with me as her star witness."

Jasmine's face registered a tidal wave of anger and surprise. "But if he does leave me and marry her, his plans for partner are shot—"

"And if he doesn't." Madeline skillfully reminded her. "She'll cry sexual harassment—"

"And for a second time—" Jasmine choked.

"And this time, she'll have a witness." Madeline pointed both thumbs toward her chest. "Me."

"And the second time around, his bid for partner will go up in smoke, for sure," Jasmine croaked.

"But if he leaves you, it will let him keep his career." Madeline surmised. "Even though the partners may frown on office romances, if they choose to put the right spin on it, Dad could still make partner, after all."

"Then it's over." Jasmine slumped into herself. "Dex made his choice to put his career—and his other women—before me long time ago."

"It's not your fault, Mom." Madeline held onto her mother's quaking form as she sobbed openly. "Dad needs help. He thinks this is nothing. He thinks he's done nothing wrong. He says having sex with these white women is just his way of sticking it to the *Man*."

"What *Man*?" Jasmine sniveled.

"White men! All white men—friends and foes, alike. He thinks all of them are out to get him, and he's sticking it to their women, not as an act of love, but as an act of revenge." Madeline threw up her hands. "Like I said, Mom, the man needs help."

"Oh, Madeline, I don't know what to do." Jasmine sounded desperate. "All my life, I've been trying to hold our family...my marriage together. I've been trying to do the right thing."

Madeline breathed a wry chuckle. "Dad's holding you hostage with that Bible stuff, Mom."

"What?" Jasmine said vaguely.

"Don't you see?" Madeline held onto her mother's shoulders. "He figures no matter what he does, you've got to forgive him; you've got to turn the other cheek."

"What are you saying?" Jasmine puzzled.

"But evil people always go too far." Madeline released her. "'Cause even the Bible allows you a divorce for adultery, doesn't it?"

"Divorce?" Jasmine shuddered.

"Yes, Mom, that's what we're talking about here." Madeline blared. "And by the looks of it, Dad's been whoring around for a long time."

"Madeline!" Jasmine drew back her hand. "I will not have you speaking about your father like that!"

"Facts, Mother! Truth!" Madeline lowered her voice, and Jasmine lowered her hand. "Somebody needs to tell it."

Jasmine sighed. "But—"

"It takes two people to be married, Mom." They settled back down on the couch. "You can't be married by yourself. You can't put the whole thing on your back and carry it around like a cross."

"But—"

"One person using the other; one person taking advantage of the other, that's not marriage." Madeline seethed. "That's madness!"

"But how will I face our friends?" Jasmine fiddled with the small cross at her neck. "How will I face my church? Everyone thinks we have the perfect marriage."

"Life is what it is, Mom; not what we want it to be." Madeline soothed. "And it doesn't matter what people think, at your church or otherwise."

"But we've been studying marriage in my Bible Study—"

"Trust me; those ladies have their own issues. They're probably not telling you the truth, either." Madeline huffed. "Here you are trying to impress them when they're probably too stressed out with their own problems to even give a care about yours."

"But the sisters in my prayer circle—"

"I'm not saying you shouldn't pray together, Mom." Madeline explained. "But I am saying I bet everyone's not coming clean. And if you can't share the truth with these ladies, are they really your friends? And if they can't accept the truth and support you in your troubles, are they really your sisters?"

"Madeline, you just don't understand—"

"Mom, I know you think I'm a still a little girl, but I'm not. I've been watching you and Dad do this dance a long time. I didn't really know he was cheating on you until I saw it with my own eyes, but I did know something was up." She breathed deeply to slow her pace. "And I know you thought I hated you and the church, but I don't. I just want you to be for real, Mom. I want you to face the truth and quit play-acting."

"And what is the truth?" Jasmine squirmed. "I don't know anymore."

"You're always telling me to pray." Madeline sulked. "But have you been talking to the Lord?"

"Madeline?" Jasmine's eyes blinked.

"Have you really been listening to what He's saying to you, trying to show you, trying to protect you from?" Madeline whined. "Mom, you've got to let this go."

"I've been holding on so long; I don't know if I can let go."

"Mom, if the bruises could show, wouldn't you let go?"

"I-I guess so." Jasmine dribbled.

"Well, aren't these bruises just as bad, Mom?" Madeline took hold of her mother's trembling hands. "And if you don't let go, it'll tear you to pieces."

"I'm so tired, Madeline." Jasmine sagged. "I feel like I've been trying to hold onto something that's been falling down around me for a long time."

"Then let it go, Mom." Madeline pleaded.

"But doesn't the Lord want families to stay together?" Jasmine's tears caught in her throat.

"Yes, Mom." Madeline flustered. "But it's the Lord who builds the house; keeps the city—not us. Isn't that what you've always told me? Isn't that what you believe?"

"Yes, but—"

"Mom, I hear you saying, 'If it can't be the way I want it to be, then I might as well give up.'" Madeline flailed her hands. "Do you think God wants you to kill yourself trying to make your dreams come true, or to live the life He's put right in front of you?"

"'Run the race that's set before us with patience.'" Jasmine quoted through her tears.

"I don't know the Bible verses, Mom." Madeline smarted. "That's your department. All I know is you can die trying to have it your way, or you can live the life you've been given. Those are the only two choices we get."

Jasmine drooped in defeat. She couldn't silence the truth ringing in her ears. Now that her daughter had seen the worse, she had a right to know—everything. "Truth be told, this has been coming for a long time, Madeline." Jasmine wiped her tears and tried to regain her dignity.

"What, Mom?"

Jasmine pushed back her frazzled hair. "I guess I just never wanted to admit it."

"What?"

Jasmine resettled herself on the couch. "When your dad met me, I was in pre-med and getting ready to graduate and move on to med school in California."

"I know." Madeline sighed. "I've heard this story a hundred times."

"But not the whole story." Jasmine shifted, avoiding her daughter's eyes. "And before you pass judgment on your dad, you need to hear it."

"O-kay."

"I got pregnant, Madeline." Jasmine explained. "I told Dex I was pregnant."

"With me?"

"No," Jasmine said. "I told him the day after I got the acceptance letter to med school at Cal, my senior year."

"What happened?"

"Your dad had gotten accepted to the U of M law school around the same time."

"That would've been quite a long-distance romance—California to Michigan."

"That's right." Jasmine nodded, remembering her whirlwind of emotions at the time. "And I told myself I'd rather marry your dad than pursue my medical career."

"So...was that the truth?" Madeline tried to preempt her disclosure.

"No." Jasmine sagged. "As much as I hate to admit it…I was just plain scared."

"That's not a big deal. I bet most people are—"

"But I made choices, Madeline, based on my fears, rather than pursuing my dreams."

"What?"

Jasmine felt like she was drowning. The weight of her confession was about to take her under. "You see, Madeline, I told your dad I was pregnant…but I was not."

"What?" Madeline's eyes startled wide open. She was prepared for any revelation, but not this one.

"We loved each other." Jasmine explained. "I knew he would do the right thing. I knew he'd marry me and take me with him to Ann Arbor rather than me having to go it alone in California."

"I thought the purpose of marriage was to fulfill each other, not to fool each other." Madeline snapped.

"Yes, I was wrong, Madeline," Jasmine whispered. She almost couldn't bear the hurt in her daughter's eyes. She thought it might swallow her up, but she pressed on. "Even though my grades and my smarts had gotten me accepted to med school, I couldn't even imagine being successful. Not me. So I lied, and we were married." Her voice dropped. "I'm sorry, Madeline."

"But the baby?" Madeline squeaked.

"I compounded the lie after we were married, when a few months later, I told Dex I had a miscarriage." Tears formed in Jasmine's eyes. They were for her darling daughter, not for herself. "Dex was disappointed, of course, but we were so happy, somehow it didn't really matter."

"But Dad didn't really want to get married, did he?"

"No, not then. And neither did I, not really." Jasmine spoke softly. "But, Madeline, all these years later, I think I hid behind the pregnancy and the marriage, rather than admit to myself…I was scared to death of being a flop at med school."

"But why, Mom? You're so smart—"

"I was smart, true. But my Mom had me when she was only 15 years old—"

"What?"

"I don't talk about it much; I was raised by your Grandma Mae. And deep inside somewhere I always felt like that unwanted kid. I didn't really feel like I was…worthy…of being a doctor, much less had what it took to succeed. I worked hard, not because I believed I'd succeed, but because I didn't."

"But it wasn't true—"

"No." Jasmine admitted. "Maybe not. But that's how I felt…deep down. My motives got all mixed-up, so I guess I opted to hide out in my marriage, my family…even my religion."

"What?"

"I convinced myself I was trying to hold our family together for the Lord." Jasmine touched her cross. "And I fooled myself into thinking I deserved whatever your daddy dished out…to make up for the lie I told him. But now I realize, I really took all of his mess out of…fear—fear of loss, fear of failure, fear of being alone—like that little girl with no mother growing up in my Grandma Mae's back bedroom."

Madeline fell back onto the sofa. She felt like she'd been sucker punched. "So then what happened," she said weakly.

"We were married. I helped your dad get through law school and pass the bar. And along the way, I became a registered nurse instead of a doctor."

"So what did Dad think about that?"

"He accepted my decision, but—"

"But—"

"But I think when I turned down my acceptance to med school at the University of California, I started to…shrink…in his eyes, and in my own. Because I had let fear rule my life, I was never the same. And your dad, I think he saw it as a failing in me—a character flaw. I was a far cry from the image he held of his darling mother, and somewhere deep inside, he began to hate me for it."

"Did he find out about the baby?"

"No. He never did." Jasmine quaked. "But there would be no lawyer *and* doctor in the house as he had planned. And little by little, he began to withdraw his love from me."

Madeline's eyes widened. "And because of that, you let him treat you any kinda way?"

"Pretty much." Jasmine's body drooped, remembering all of the things Dex probably held against her. "Settling…cost me my dream, my edge, myself…and my husband's respect. All these years, I've been trying to regain his favor…his love—"

"But at what cost, Mother?" Madeline exclaimed.

"I'm beginning to understand that now, Madeline." Jasmine nodded. "The price I've paid is much too high. Believe me. I know."

"So what will you do now?"

Jasmine sniffed. "I don't know." She admitted flatly. "All these years of trying to please Dex, I somehow went past myself. I took so much stuff I didn't believe in, I lost myself. I don't really know who I am anymore. I don't know what I like. I don't know what I want. Oh, Madeline—"

"It's alright, Mom." Madeline smoothed the back of her hand. "One step at a time."

Jasmine straightened. "Hopefully, I've taken a big step today…coming clean with you…and with myself."

Madeline gave her a weak smile. "Thanks, Mom," she said, "for trusting me with the truth."

"But what about you, Madeline?"

"What about me?"

"You and your dad—"

"Dad is Dad, Mom. I've known that for a long time. Not to worry. I'll handle my relationship with my Dad. I'll be fine, Mom. We…will be fine, Mom." Madeline hugged her mother tightly. There was nothing standing between them anymore.

CHAPTER 33
Leeza

"Dad!" Leeza's throat tensed as she turned her key in his front door. "We're here." Detective Visclosky and his team were on her heels, and she was fearful what their intrusion might do to her dad's fragile state of health. This whole mix-up—the audacity of disturbing her mother's gravesite—had caused him great distress.

"I don't want you here." Lee Manchester mumbled from his chair in the kitchen. "But you're here, so come in." He growled. He was wearing his full oxygen mask for the occasion; not a good sign. And if his rheumy eyes and pasty white skin were any indication, he was having a bad day.

"How're you feeling, Dad?" Leeza said sweetly. "This is Detective Visclosky and his team. They're here to…execute the search warrant I told you about. Remember?"

"Of course, I remember," her dad said hoarsely. "I've got a bad ticker. I'm not senile!"

"Okay, Dad," Leeza whispered. "This will go a lot quicker if you just calm down and breathe."

"I am breathing, blast you! I just don't want all these people tramping through my house."

Detective Visclosky moved closer to his chair. "We'll be quick, sir, and careful."

Leeza whispered to the detective, "My Dad rarely throws anything away, so all of my Mom's things are probably still upstairs in the master bedroom. Dad moved his bedroom down here to avoid the stairs."

"Why're you whispering?" Lee Manchester puffed. "I'm well within my rights to know everything that happens in my own home."

"And so you are, sir." Detective Visclosky handed him the search warrant. "This is for your review, Mr. Manchester," he said. "It permits us to search the premises—the house, garage, out-buildings and the grounds. As Miss Manchester has informed you, we're looking for ways your wife might've been exposed to the poison that compromised her system."

"Yeah-Yeah! Leeza told me, but I still think it's a crock!" Lee Manchester blustered. "My wife, bless her soul, died in an unfortunate plane crash…and that's the beginning and end of it."

"Yes, sir," the detective said as he signaled his team to move out and do their job.

"But there is some good news, Dad." Leeza eased in.

"Not likely on a day like today." Her dad seethed, while Detective Visclosky crossed his arms and took his post against the wall.

Leeza twirled around like a ballerina to get her dad's attention. "I got it, Dad! I got it!" she said.

"You got what?" Lee Manchester bristled. "Spit it out! This is not a day for mysteries."

Leeza pulled up a chair in front of him and let her knees touch his. "I got what you wanted, Dad." She smiled. "I got…blue chipper number three!"

"You what?" Her dad's face mask fogged over. "You won, my Sweet-Girl? You won the contest?"

"Yes, Dad." Leeza cheered. "I did!"

"I knew you could do it, Sweet-Girl!" Manchester was close to tears. "I knew you could do it!"

"I haven't had a chance to tell Mr. Cole yet, but I signed-on Sebatha Enterprises yesterday. That's why I was able to get back here from London to be with you."

If her dad could've managed it in his weakened state, he would've stuck out his chest. Instead, he said, "Detective, I'll have you know I, Lee Manchester, made it possible for my daughter to go to the finest schools. I…was here to greet her every day when she came home from school. I…took her to all her practices and all her meets. It was my hard work that made her the success she is today."

"Impressive." Detective Visclosky fished for the proper response.

"Dad, the detective isn't interested in our ancient history." Leeza protested. "Besides, Mom had a lot to do with—"

"Your mom was never here, Leeza." Lee Manchester wheezed. "She was off making a name for herself in the publishing world. I…was here for you. I…made sure you didn't waste your talent and your life being some unknown starving artist in SoHo."

"That's not fair, Dad." Leeza argued. "You were only here because you got too sick to follow your career—"

"I was not too sick." Manchester snarled. "I just had a bad ticker. I could've pursued my career if your mother had given me her full support. But, no, she craved the limelight and her own success more." He coughed. "And what of you if I had pursued my career? Your mother wasn't willing to give up her pursuits to attend to you—"

"My Mother loved me!" Leeza protested. "You faulted Mom because you were a good architect, but not a great one. But it was Mom who tucked me in at night. She read me stories and played dress up with me. She listened to me when I told her that I wanted to paint. She supported my dreams to be an artist. She bought me supplies. She—"

"Rubbish!" Manchester coughed. "All rubbish!"

"We've got everything we need from upstairs, Detective." One of his men broke in.

"Then fan out." Detective Visclosky signaled. This was a conversation he didn't want to miss.

"Don't you see, Leeza? Your success proves me right." Her dad persisted. "With your brains and your connections, you beat that Kyle-nobody. And this promotion will be your first of many more to come; just you wait and see."

Leeza retreated. She was growing weary of the constant battle over how they remembered the past. "If you say so, Dad." She retorted. "But if it weren't for my painting, I'd have no peace at all. And as for this job, it just might be demanding more of me than I'm willing to give."

"I doubt that." Her dad huffed. "You're my Little Trooper; you'll stick it out."

"Detective." The sergeant called. "Can you step this way?"

"Coming." Detective Visclosky excused himself and followed the sergeant to the garage.

The sergeant showed him a plain brown wrapped package. "We found this in the greenhouse," he said.

"What is it?" The detective peered into the bag.

"Well, my Taiwanese is pretty rusty." The sergeant kidded. "But I'm told this is a box of arsenic poison."

"What's it used for?" Detective Visclosky pressed.

"Most times, it's used as a pesticide." The sergeant explained. "You can get it real easy from Southeast Asia over the internet. No questions asked."

"From the looks of it, the bag's been around a while."

"Postmark on the wrapper suggests it was purchased over five years ago—"

"Right around the same time Mrs. Manchester was receiving her doses of the poison."

"Seems so." The sergeant nodded. "But if Mr. Manchester was using this on his wife, why didn't he get rid of if after her death?"

"Miss Manchester tells me her dad is something of a pack rat." The detective returned the bag. "And she tells me her dad hasn't

195

been able to move outside of the confines of the house for some years now. He can't go any further than his oxygen cord will allow. He can't even get as far as the garage."

"Makes sense." The sergeant shrugged. "Maybe Mr. Manchester wanted to destroy the evidence, but just couldn't get to it. And besides, since his wife died in a plane crash, maybe Mr. Manchester didn't see the need to get rid of the poison…until it was too late."

"This is going to be tricky." Detective Visclosky scratched his head. "I think I may have already overheard a motive. And if there's something fishy here, if Mr. Manchester did indeed poison his wife, I don't want to leave here without a confession."

"So what do you want us to do, Boss?"

"Two things." The detective gave his instructions and returned to the house.

"Is there a problem, Detective?" Leeza asked when he returned to the kitchen.

"No." The detective stated evenly. "Mr. Manchester." He continued. "When's the last time you were in your greenhouse?"

Leeza started to answer. "Oh, that's been a while—"

"I need Mr. Manchester to answer." The detective interrupted.

"Why is that important?" Manchester bristled.

"Not important." The detective smiled. "Just a question I need answered, sir."

"Let me see." Lee Manchester reseated his face mask and took a peek at Leeza. "I've been tied to this blasted oxygen compressor for three years, so it had to be before that."

Leeza giggled, trying to lighten the mood. "Dad can only venture as far as his oxygen cord will let him."

"So you said." The detective reminded her they'd had this conversation earlier in the car.

"So were you having trouble with mice or other pests back then, sir?"

"Could've been." Manchester clipped. "Don't remember."

"Dad used to have a marvelous garden out back—roses, caladiums, azaleas—"

"The detective is not interested in all that, Leeza." Her dad interrupted.

"So, since you can't get out." The detective stalled. "How do you get your groceries, your supplies?"

"As you know, Detective, we can get everything we need online these days." Manchester spouted. "I'm sure that comes as no surprise to you."

"No, sir. No surprise." Detective Visclosky took up his position on the wall. "I just wondered how you did it."

"My daughter, here, sees to it that I have around-the-clock care if I need it," Manchester said loftily. "But I prefer to do as much as I can. That's how I keep myself going."

"I understand, sir."

"So what is the point of this conversation?" Leeza queried. "My Dad is tired, so if you've gotten what you came for, it's best that we go now."

"I thought your lawyer was coming, Miss Manchester?" the detective said.

"She is." Leeza checked her watch. "Don't know what could be holding her up. But as I said, we don't have to wait for her if you've completed your work here."

"Just one more thing." Detective Visclosky eased in. "Did you buy the arsenic poison in your greenhouse on-line, Mr. Manchester?"

Lee Manchester choked, and Leeza leapt forward to help revive him. "Can't you see he's a sick man?" Leeza pleaded. "Can't this wait?"

"No, ma'am. It can't." The detective stood at attention. "If you're okay, now, Mr. Manchester, can you please answer my question."

"I...I bought it for the rats." Manchester sputtered. "For the rats."

"Then why didn't you get rid of it when you got rid of the rats?" Detective Visclosky pressed. "We didn't find any evidence of rodents in your garage or your greenhouse."

"My Dad doesn't throw things away." Leeza appealed to the detective with her eyes. "He's frugal like that. I told you."

"Yes, Miss. You did." The detective leveled her with his eyes.

"What does it matter anyway?" Lee Manchester recovered. "I wouldn't have known how to dispose of it properly."

"Good answer." Detective Visclosky granted. "That's why I've had my man run it over to the Pennsylvania Highway Patrol lab. Got a friend over there who owes me a favor."

"What?" Leeza sagged.

"I should be hearing from him any minute now," the detective said. "Miss Manchester, you might want to call your lawyer and get her over here."

"Lawyer?" Lee Manchester prickled. "I don't need a lawyer."

"Dad." Leeza pleaded. "Just stop talking until Annibelle gets here. You remember her. We played lacrosse at Yale together."

"These officers have nothing on me, Leeza." Manchester steadied. "And I don't need a lawyer."

Detective Visclosky stepped into the den to take a call, and the room was put on pause. When he stepped back into the kitchen he said, "Got some news from the lab, Mr. Manchester. But is there anything you want to tell me first?"

Lee Manchester coughed and stuck out his chin with all the energy he could muster. "Yes," he said. "I tried to kill her."

"What?" Leeza gasped and fell into a chair. And in that moment, she caught a flash of her dad in the kitchen on the day of the plane crash. It had always struck her as odd that he would choose that time to pour the apple juice down the drain—the juice that only her mother drank.

"Yes, I did my very best to kill that witch." Lee Manchester hissed. "Because she had everything I wanted. And if I couldn't have it, I wanted to give it to Leeza." He croaked in his face mask. "In fact, I felt a little cheated when the airplane crash beat me to it!"

"Dad? Leeza gurgled. "You tried to kill Mom? Why?"

"Your mother would've been satisfied with your being some stupid artist." Her dad sagged. "She said, 'there's nothing wrong with Leeza exploring her artistic side.' Stupid woman! She only valued her own success. Not mine! Not yours! Don't you see, Leeza?"

"But murder…Mom?" Leeza could barely speak the words.

"I did it for you because I love you." Her dad strained to catch his breath. "I wanted the best for you, like I did everyday of your life." He waved his hand weakly. "Who made you meatballs? Who kissed your boo-boos? Who helped you study?" He wheezed. "Not that short-sighted, self-important witch who couldn't find her way home before midnight! Not her!" Manchester's hands shook violently. "Me!"

"Calm down, Mr. Manchester." Detective Visclosky cautioned. "You might want to wait for your lawyer."

But Lee Manchester was on a roll. "Leeza," he said weakly, "I wanted you to be able to go to the best schools, so you could have the career I could only dream of. And if I couldn't afford to send you…the life insurance money from your mother's death surely could." He coughed deeply. "Did you know her office gave her a five million dollar policy?"

"Oh, Dad!" Leeza ran for the bathroom before she lost her lunch in front of everyone. It was becoming so clear why he always tried to push out the mother she loved—out of her memories, out of her heart.

"We're placing you under arrest, Mr. Manchester." Detective Visclosky announced. "You have the right to remain silent. You have the right—"

Lee Manchester collapsed before they could get him in handcuffs, and an emergency call was placed to the local paramedics.

CHAPTER 34
Cristal

"Pastor Gabe, thanks for seeing us." Cristal bounced into his office clutching Malik's hand. Malik simply shrugged his shoulders at Pastor Gabe because Cristal hadn't told him the purpose for their visit. He knew she was up to something, but she hadn't shared with him the events of the previous day—her meeting with Daddy-Travis, or her blow up with Chantilly.

Pastor Gabe, ever the gentleman, said, "Please, come in; have a seat, you two."

"I hate I had to be so mysterious with your secretary, Pastor." Cristal admitted. "But there was just no way to prepare you, or Malik, for what I have to say." Cristal took one seat and Malik the other. This time, she scooted her chair close to his and continued to hold onto his hand.

Pastor Gabe was dumbfounded by her new tune, but he played along. "So…how're the children," he said.

"I wanted babies." Cristal giggled. "Now, we've got four of 'em." She squeezed Malik's hand.

"And how's that working out for you two?" Pastor Gabe folded his brow.

Cristal continued to do all the talking because her change in attitude had left Malik at a loss for words. "I love Chanel's kids so much," she said, "and who would've thought I'd ever get a chance to help raise them?" She smiled lovingly at Malik. "I was running around trying to have a baby my own way, when the Lord had this in mind for us all along. And me and Malik, getting a chance to raise these kids we've known since they were born, is so very special for us."

"Well, that's real good." Pastor Gabe looked at Malik for confirmation. Malik smiled and nodded his agreement.

"I hope Chanel will get better real soon," Cristal continued, "but we'll always have a part in these kid's lives. We'll never forget them, and they'll never forget us. And besides, by them living with us, we can make sure they get to meet Jesus in Sunday School and church."

"So is that why you brought us here today, Cristal, to discuss our mutual good fortune?" Pastor Gabe said.

"Nope." Cristal scooted her chair even closer to Malik and squeezed his hand until it lost circulation. "It's a little more complicated than that."

"What then?" Pastor Gabe pressed. "Tell me what's on your mind."

Cristal loosed Malik's hand, reached into her MK tote, and pulled out an envelope.

Malik sat up straighter in his chair and stared at her. "What's that?" he asked.

"It's a letter," she said. "Written a long time ago...by my Father."

"Huh?" Malik's jaw clenched. "And you didn't tell me about it?"

"I just received it yesterday." Cristal's eyes misted. "It was a secret letter...but it seems all the secrets are out now."

"What does the letter say?" Pastor Gabe inquired.

"Dunno." Cristal admitted. "With all that went on yesterday, I didn't have the strength to read it—not alone."

"Are you going to read it to us?" Pastor Gabe said.

"Yes," Cristal said. "I waited to read it with you and Malik—the ones I love, and the ones I know love me—'cause y'all have put up with a lot o' my mess." Her eyes glistened as she looked at her husband and her pastor. "But first let me say who I got it from," she said.

"Who?" Malik encouraged. He was so glad to see his wife acting like her old self again.

"Uncle Travis."

"Uncle Travis?" Malik bristled. "He held your letter all these years? Why?"

Cristal's hand trembled as she opened the envelope. "Malik, you went to see Uncle Travis because you were concerned about me—about how Chantilly was dogging me out," she said. "And he thought it was time for me to read this letter from my Father."

"Then let's read it, by all means." Pastor Gabe urged.

Cristal unfolded the letter that was typed on Travis Johnson's letterhead and read: "My dear, darling daughter, Cristal. Let me start by saying I love you very much. You have always been a joy and a delight to me, from the day you were born until this present time. If you're reading this, I've gone on to glory, but please take comfort in knowing my love for you will never die." Cristal raised her head and batted away her tears. Malik put a comforting hand on her thigh.

Cristal continued reading. "I've asked your Uncle Travis to hold this letter back from you, unless you needed to know the contents in order to deal more effectively with your mother. I have always loved your mother, but I realize that she can be more than a handful at times. And I do not want her terrible secret to become a problem for you when I am no longer around to defend you." Cristal's breath caught in her throat. "You see, Cristal, my dear, sweet daughter, I am not your 'biological' father."

Malik and Pastor Gabe bolted upright. They shared glances and then flashed on Cristal. "Are you all right?" Malik put his arms around her. "Is this some sort of joke?" he asked.

"Or mistake?" Pastor Gabe added.

Cristal shook them off. She didn't want to lose her nerve. "Just let me finish," she whispered. "And I think you'll understand."

"Okay." They quieted.

Cristal continued reading her father's letter. "And please keep in mind, my dear, I have known this all along; almost, from the moment of your birth. But, rest assured, it didn't matter to me; it never mattered to me. You are my sweet, little girl, and that is all that has ever mattered to me. But your Uncle Travis and I have DNA results to prove my claim."

"DNA?" Malik interrupted. "Then you know for certain?" He flapped.

Cristal sighed and continued. "My dear, Cristal, I regret that I am unable to tell you who your biological father is. Chantilly never owned-up to her misdeed. She couldn't admit it to herself, and I found myself unable to discuss it with her. I did not want to push her into taking her frustrations out on you. I did not want to cause her further distress. I love your mother."

Cristal breathed. "I've left this letter in your Uncle Travis' safe keeping, to be shared with you only in the event it would be of benefit to you. That's it, my dear Cristal. Do not ever allow your mother to bully you or cause you distress. I have made provisions for you and Chanel that do not require her involvement. I have made you independent young women. Use it to your advantage. And may God be with you and keep you always. You have my deepest and sincerest love, Your Father." The letter was signed in Morgan Moore's own hand.

Malik and Pastor Gabe were speechless. Malik was the first to find his voice. "Are you all right, Cris?" He whispered. "Are you all right, Babe?"

"Yes, my dear sister," Pastor Gabe added. "Are you okay with this knowledge?"

A vague smile crept across Cristal's face. "The letter would've come as a complete shock to me, too," she said, "if I didn't already know the rest of the story—"

"The rest of the story?" Malik pressed. "What's the rest of the story?"

"I also found out who my real Daddy is yesterday." Cristal's smile blossomed. "And I had it out with Chantilly, too."

"My Lord!" Pastor Gabe exclaimed. "You've been through so much in such a short time—"

"It's all good, Pastor." Cristal relieved him. "I'm cool with it."

Malik turned Cristal to face him. "So who is your real daddy, Babe?"

Cristal was chuckling, now. "You won't believe it," she said. "It's Uncle Travis!"

Malik shot up like a bullet. "Uncle Travis?" He nearly screamed.

"Yes." Cristal confirmed. "He and Chantilly had a one-night affair…and up popped me!"

"I can't believe it." Malik was slack jawed. He dropped back into his chair. "Your prissy mama—"

"Believe it," Cristal said. "Uncle Travis—my Daddy—told me so when he gave me the letter yesterday; and then I went over and had it out with Chantilly. She had to upchuck the truth."

"Wow!" was all Malik could manage.

Pastor Gabe added. "The Lord works in mysterious ways—"

"You're so right, Pastor." Cristal went around his desk and hugged his neck. "There were so many things I couldn't see. I didn't know the people around me—the people I loved and wanted to love me—had so many…mixed-up motives…that had nothing at all to do with me."

"We can never know everything, Sis. Cristal." Pastor Gabe smiled broadly. "That's why we have to trust the Lord."

"I wanted babies. He gave us not one, but four." Cristal squeezed both of Malik's hands. "I wanted love. He gave me truth." She teared up. "I accepted Jesus a long time ago as my Saviour. Now, I trust Him as my Lord," she said. "He knows things I don't know. He does things I can't do. His timing is perfect. He's in charge—and not me—"

"You're so right." Pastor Gabe nodded. "This very day has been coming since God made it in the six days. And if you'll trust Him in it—and not in your own efforts—then you're ready—"

"Ready for what, Pastor?" Malik and Cristal spoke as one.

"Ready to start living in the seventh day!"

CHAPTER 35
Jasmine

Jasmine was clicking off her cellphone call when Madeline saddled up alongside her at the kitchen counter. "How are you, Mom?"

"Hmm." Jasmine gave it some thought. "I was going back and forth for a while. But I think I'm better now…much better."

"That's good to hear," Madeline said. "Because Spring Break is over, and I've got to head back to D.C."

Jasmine reached out and smoothed her daughter's hand. "I know, Baby," she said, "and I'm glad. It's time for you to get back to your own life."

"But I hate leaving you like this—"

"Not to worry." Jasmine assured her with a look. "I'll be just fine. I think I'm finally learning what the Lord's been trying to teach me—"

"Which is—" Madeline gestured for her mother to continue.

"Which is…we can't avoid trouble, Madeline." Jasmine sighed. "Trouble is a fact of life. Everybody's got it—some have one thing, and some another. It just is. And no amount of lying or trying can hold it back." Jasmine smiled. "But the Lord is right here with us, and He'll help us through it all…no matter what."

Madeline squeezed her hand. "Sounds like to me you've come a long way in the few days I've been home."

Jasmine hugged herself. "On that worst night," she said, "that dark night after your dad left me; that night you spent in the hotel; that night I was swallowed up with grief. I was crying out to the Lord and straining to hold onto my sanity. I was hurting so bad; I thought I'd go mad."

"Oh, Mom—"

"No." Jasmine shushed her. "Let me finish," she said. "I nearly died that night because I thought my failed marriage meant I had failed God; that I'd broken my vow to Him. But He let me know, He holds me up…I don't hold Him up."

"How?"

Jasmine sat up straighter. "That night…when I felt my mind slipping into nothingness…I heard the Spirit whisper, 'Come this way. Come this way. Trust in Me. Lean on Me.'"

"And then what happened?" Madeline gasped.

"My heart slowed; my mind caught hold." Jasmine's smile brightened. "And a peace came over me…and I knew…the Lord will never let me fall."

"I'm so glad, Mom." Madeline nodded.

"And since you've gotten me straight about some things, too, my wise Baby-Girl," Jasmine said, "I'm starting to feel one with myself, again." She gleamed at her daughter. "Jesus loves me more than anything He'll ever give me, or anything He'll ever take away. And I love Him more than anything or anybody." She squeezed her daughter's hand. "And He wants you to trust Him like that, too, Madeline."

"I do, Mom." Madeline beamed. "All I've ever wanted was for you to get to know the real me and for you to be alright."

"I'm getting there." Jasmine winked.

"And what about the church folk—your friends?" Madeline's nostrils flared. "All the people you've been so worried about knowing your business?"

Jasmine pursed her lips. "The people who love me will love me. And the ones who don't…won't."

"Good answer." Madeline glimmered. "So…have you talked to Dad lately?" She pointed to Jasmine's cellphone.

"Nope. That wasn't your dad on the line. That was a friend I met at the Atlanta airport during Hurricane Allee…and she's going through some things, too." Jasmine shrugged. "Your dad hasn't called me since he moved out, and I have no reason to call him."

"Then I hate to be the bearer of bad tidings." Madeline slowed. "But Dad has filed for divorce. You'll probably be served with the papers soon."

"Figured as much when you told me it was either divorce me or keep his job." Jasmine sipped her coffee. "There was no doubt in my mind he'd choose his job."

"And that heifer, Nicole, is pressuring him to do it sooner than later." Madeline flustered. "She keeps reminding him that I'm the star witness for her sexual harassment case should he try to back out of the deal. And she said to me—" Madeline mimicked Nicole's Jersey-girl accent. "If your dad doesn't wanna have you commuting from D.C. to Dallas for the trial of the century, he'd better get on with the divorce and set our wedding date—and soon.'"

"She had the nerve to say that to you?" Jasmine bristled.

"Yep." Madeline waved it off. "But not to worry. That silly, little tart doesn't faze me. I've had dealings with her before. She thinks she's Dad's gatekeeper, or something."

"Then I guess Nicole is satisfied just to have the man." Jasmine sniffed. "Even though she's got to know in her heart that Dex loves his career, and not her."

"Yes, but I think she's okay with that, Mom." Madeline smirked. "If you ask me, that white chick is about the money and the notoriety she thinks she'll get by being Mrs. Dexter Davis."

Jasmine raised her brows. "Sounds like a match made in hell."

"Pretty much." Madeline agreed. "And it appears to me like Dad doesn't have much of a say in the matter. He's like a spider, trapped in his own stupid web."

"Then—" Jasmine exhaled. "I guess the next time I'll see your dad is in court."

"Get yourself a good lawyer, Mom." Madeline advised. "One that's not hooked into Dad or his firm in any way."

"I will." Jasmine agreed. "I may not be able to look out for my own best interests where Dex is concerned, but I'll certainly get a lawyer who can." She shrugged. "Twenty-five years of marriage has got to be worth something."

"Good." Madeline got up and hugged her mom. "Then I'll go pack. I'm leaving you in good hands."

"About that." Jasmine returned her hug. "I don't want this divorce…or Miss Nicole…or anything…to come between you and your dad."

"Not to worry, Mom." Madeline headed out of the kitchen. "I'm a daddy's girl. And I know better than to choose sides in 'grown folks' business." She gave a sassy flip at the door. "And besides, what Dad's getting himself into, I wouldn't wish on a dog. Trust me. It's got its own reward."

Jasmine waved as her daughter turned the corner. "Glad to get to know you, my wise, Baby-Girl."

CHAPTER 36
Leeza

Leeza was a wreck. Amid the sirens and flashing lights and heroic attempts, the paramedics had not been able to revive her father. He'd died in her arms while in police custody for the attempted murder of her mother, and she had a funeral to plan. If that wasn't enough, it was the end of February, and she needed to meet with her boss. She needed to tell Mr. Cole, face-to-face, that she'd gotten her third blue chipper, which made her first in-line to take his seat upon his inevitable promotion to partner. And she didn't want her rival, Kyle, to beat her to the finish line.

With all the pressure building, Leeza didn't know which to do first, scream or lose her mind. So she took Jasmine's advice, and she prayed. Their long conversation on her flight back from London had finally led her to the place of faith. And she poured out her heart to the Lord—all of her frustrations and all of her intense disappointments. It took a while, but it was the only way she could stay sane. The funeral arrangements couldn't wait, so they came next. Her office sent the biggest wreath to the small ceremony, and red-headed Kyle attended the service, too. But after less than a week of mourning, Leeza dried her eyes and called Mr. Cole's secretary for an appointment the next day.

Dick Cole was rubbing his greedy, little palms together when Leeza crossed his threshold. "Come in, Miss Manchester," he said like she was Queen Victoria. "Great to see you back. It is the month of March, you know. Take a seat."

Leeza was wearing a black sheath and sunglasses. She did as she was told. "Good afternoon, Mr. Cole." She laid her Prada bag at her feet. "And, yes, I'm keenly aware; this is the long-awaited month of March.

"So sorry about your father." Cole pretended to care. "I want you to consider us your family here at Bradford and Baker, and whatever you need, you have but to ask."

"I do." Leeza pretended to believe him. "I will."

"Can I have Mary bring you something?" Cole took a sip from his stained mug.

"No." Leeza spoke confidently. "Thank you, sir. I'm fine."

"Then what is the purpose of your visit today, Miss Manchester," Cole said hopefully. "I understand you made a trip to London before your father's untimely demise."

"I did." Leeza removed her sunglasses to reveal her bloodshot eyes. "And it was very productive," she said.

"Productive, indeed?" Mr. Cole parroted.

"I used my connections." Leeza breathed. "I used all of my assets to sign-up—Sebatha Enterprises—my third blue chipper from your secret list, Mr. Cole."

Cole could no longer hide his enthusiasm. "I told you, Miss Manchester!" He cheered. "I told you my money was on you to win this race." He glowed over her. "And look at you, my dear, you've done just that." He buzzed his secretary. "Mary, bring us two glasses of chilled champagne...pronto!"

Leeza placed her hands in her lap. "So I presume Kyle has not yet snagged his third client."

"He has not." Cole beamed. "I told you he'd have a struggle with the Fairchild Group. They don't trust anybody over there who hasn't played lacrosse at Yale or Harvard." Cole snickered. "And as we well know, Kyle is a far cry from those circles."

"So when will you hear about your bid for partner, Mr. Cole?" Leeza took the offensive.

Cole breathed a sigh of relief. "It's been rather touch and go, Miss Manchester; what with me not knowing whether or not you would achieve your mission." He chuckled. "But the Partner's

Selection Panel meets early next week. And with these five, new blue-chip clients in my portfolio, I'm sure to be a shoe-in for partner!" He lowered his tone. "So this means me, you, and Kyle will have to keep this under our hats until then." He looked bothered. "Can you do that?"

"Of course, Mr. Cole," Leeza said smugly. "But will you tell Kyle of my latest conquest?"

"No!" Cole blared. "No need making him jealous and reckless when I'm so close to the finished line. We'll let this be our little secret, Leeza." He recovered quickly. "You haven't told him, have you? I know he attended your father's funeral."

"No, Mr. Cole. I didn't tell him," Leeza said. "I wanted you to be the first to know. And I wanted to tell you face-to-face." She lowered her chin. "Because I wanted to hear you say to me, face-to-face, that you will make me your successor when you become partner."

"Of course, Leeza." Cole traded his coffee mug for the champagne flute his secretary offered him. "That goes without saying."

Leeza waved off the champagne and rose to leave. "Then I have your word."

"Yes, Miss Manchester." Cole toasted himself. "You have my word."

***

It was a blustering March day when the Partner's Selection Panel convened behind closed doors for their final meeting. The days since Leeza informed her boss that she had snagged her third blue chipper had passed slowly, and she had tried to avoid Kyle at all cost. Leeza wasn't good at lying, and she didn't want to be dishonest with Kyle about her success. He'd shown sincere concern over the circumstances surrounding her father's death. But this was the long-awaited day, and the whole company seemed to be on pause; even the elevators weren't moving between floors.

The partner's Chief of Staff heaved open the doors of the conference room on the 75th floor and made an impromptu announcement. "It's Cole!" he said excitedly. "Cole is the new partner!"

"And who's his replacement?" Some brave soul asked from the back hallway.

"Brandi Mason." He boasted. "She was the unanimous choice of the partners, including their newest member, Mr. Richard *Dick* Cole."

Everyone who'd gathered like vultures waiting on the news sauntered away as though the outcome was anticlimactic. The office pool had odds on Cole becoming the new partner, anyhow. But Leeza was aghast. She ran the stairs to Kyle's office to see if he was in, only to find him sitting at his desk with his head in his hands.

"Kyle!" Leeza exploded. "Did you hear the announcement?"

"No." He moaned. "But I can pretty much imagine the results."

"Snap out of it, Kyle!" Leeza took a seat at his desk. "You don't have to imagine anymore. It's out now. It wasn't the official announcement, but it's good enough."

"Then what is it?" Kyle raised his heavy head.

"Cole made partner." Leeza ran her fingers through her short blonde curls. Since her dad's funeral, she'd ditched her flat irons and her severe pageboy and let her natural curls flow.

"Our boss? Swell." Kyle feigned a yawn. "He just should've...since I heard through the grapevine you got your third blue chipper right on time, Leeza." He faced her. "But I should've heard it from you."

"You're right, Kyle." Leeza's head drooped. "I should've told you, but Cole swore me to secrecy."

"And how's that working out for you?" Kyle's eyes flamed.

Leeza sighed heavily. "Not too well, I'm afraid."

Kyle's ears perked up. "Why? What happened?"

"After all that head pounding and jet lag, and—" Leeza stopped herself. "I nearly had to give up my body for this job, Kyle." She admitted. "And after all of that…Cole voted, along with the rest of the partners, to make Brandi Mason his replacement.

Kyle broke into insane laughter. "He did what?" He chortled. "You mean that lousy Toad E. Frog—"

"Kyle!"

Kyle toned it down for Leeza's sake. "You mean that low-down Dick Cole didn't have the balls to stand up for you, even though you're the reason for his success—"

"We…are the reason for his success, Kyle." Leeza corrected. "You and me."

"And with all we went through for that coward—all the hours, all the ring kissing." Kyle chuckled. "He still stabbed us both in the back?"

"Yes, Kyle…and I don't know what you find so funny."

"It's not funny, ha-ha, Leeza." He gathered himself. "It's funny, sad."

"Yeah, sad for both of us."

"No, Leeza." Kyle scrubbed his hands through his red hair. "Sad…for me."

"What're you saying?"

"I'm outta here, Leeza." Kyle moaned. "If Brandi Mason is our new boss, I'm as good as gone."

"But why?"

"She hates me; that's why!" Kyle shouted. "While you've been jetting all over the globe, I've been trying to make a case for getting her fired. I made a good run at it, too. I've got a file on her this thick." Kyle measured with his hands. "But now—"

"Did she know what you were doing?" Leeza quizzed.

"Did she know?" Kyle chuckled. "There're no secrets at Bradford, Baker...and Cole. You know that. Of course, Brandi knows. And, now, with full access at her disposal, she'll uncover every detail of my little scheme."

"Oh, Kyle." Leeza reached out to him. "What can we do?"

"You don't have to do anything, Leeza." Kyle stuttered. "You brought in three, new blue chippers. You're sure to keep your job, but me—"

"Kyle, I won't stay if they kick you out—"

"Yes, you will, Leeza." Kyle gave her a faint smile. "This is your career. This is your life."

"No. It's not." Leeza firmed. "I don't need this job to define me. I used to think I did, but not anymore."

"You're a beast at this job, Leeza; a natural." Kyle commended. "What's happening to your edge?"

"Been talking to a friend." Leeza confided. "She's been helping me see the light...and the seventh day."

"Huh?"

"I don't quite get it either, but I'm learning." Leeza carped. "But I know I don't want a job where they lie to your face and stab you in the back just to get ahead."

"What other kind of jobs are there." Kyle shrugged. "Sooner or later, they all treat you like dirt."

"Then I'm out of this rat race, Kyle." Leeza slapped his desk. "I quit!"

"What are you saying, Leeza." Kyle implored. "Think of all you've accomplished. Think of all you'd lose—"

"You can't lose what you don't want." Leeza bristled. "And I don't want this...not anymore!"

"But what will you do?" Kyle flapped.

"I'll paint." Passion blazed in Leeza's eyes. "It's my first love; and with my inheritance, I won't have to starve right away."

"But—"

"So I quit, Kyle…you stay. You can take my slot."

"Just because you quit, doesn't mean Witch Brandi will let me stay."

Leeza held his eyes. "Cole can make it happen. He's a partner, now. And he owes me at least that much." Leeza smiled. "Besides, Kyle, you brought in two blue chippers, too. And if things go really bad, you can drop the bomb about Brandi sleeping with the lead partner; and I'm sure Cole wouldn't want that."

Kyle moved from behind his desk and hugged Leeza tightly. "You're special," he said. "You know that?"

"I'm God's child." Leeza hugged him back. "So, yeah, I know that."

CHAPTER 37
Meeting in the Airport II
One Year Later

The ladies hugged and kissed each other on the cheeks before taking their seats at a back table in Patti's Restaurant. "Thank you, Cristal, for arranging this delicious soul food lunch for us—exactly one year from the day we first met—right here at the Atlanta Airport," Jasmine said, fanning back her tears of excitement.

"Not a problem." Cristal smiled. "Me and Patti are cool like that. And if we ain't got nothing else in the ATL, we've got some good food."

"It's so good to see you both." Leeza giggled. She looked lovely in her natural blonde curls. "And thank you, Cristal, for booking us on this seven-day Virgin Islands cruise. I'm sure we can all use the rest."

"Yep, a little fun in the sun is what we need." Cristal beamed as the waiter set out their pre-planned meals. "So before we fly out to Miami to board the ship," Cristal said, "let's catch up right here so we won't have nothing setting us off when we're in our bikinis." She grinned at Jasmine who was taking the first bite of her ribs. "You go first, Jasmine," she said.

Jasmine used her napkin. "Well," she said, "my husband, Dex, left me, and the divorce is final."

"Aww!" Cristal and Leeza fixed their faces into a little pout, but they didn't fail to notice that at 40-pounds lighter, Jasmine's cute face and her shapely legs were back in play. And if her short, little sundress was any indication of coming attractions, her new bikini was going to get lots of notice.

"No-No." Jasmine raised her hand in protest. "My marriage is over, but the Lord gave me back my life." She giggled. "So save your pity for Dex. He's got to marry his gold-digging assistant, Nicole; and from what I hear, it ain't gonna be pretty."

Leeza and Cristal snickered. "Serves him right." They agreed. "And what about you, Jasmine; what will you do?" Leeza inquired.

"I've been through so much for so long, I'm not sure what happy is for me anymore." Jasmine confided. "The loneliest I've ever been was when I was married." She sighed. "I thought I had to take anything from Dex just to make it last, and I nearly chewed off my own tongue trying to let him have his way. But, now, the Lord has taught me to always speak the truth in love and not to let anybody tap-dance on my head—not ever again."

"Here! Here!"

"So, now, I'm finding my way back to happy." Jasmine brightened. "I've always wanted to see the world. And this trip, thanks to you two ladies, will be what I hope is my first of many more to come. And Dex's big ole alimony checks will foot the bills." She winked. "Dex made partner. But with what the judge awarded me and my daughter, Madeline—she's decided to be a pharmacist, you know—I wonder if there'll be enough money left over for his new bride to get her nails done."

"Whoo-Hoo!" They all grinned. "Serves her right!"

Jasmine continued. "And I want to thank you, too, Cristal, for arranging all this." She pulled out two small, gold boxes from her bag and pushed them toward each of her friends. "A gift from me to you."

"What is it?" Cristal shook the little box. "Let me see."

"Ahh!" Leeza cooed as they opened the boxes. "Jasmine, it's a necklace—"

"A little, gold cross necklace; just like the one you wear." Cristal smiled.

"Just a lil' sumthin'-sumthin'." Jasmine teased, as each lady snapped on her necklace and set the cross in place.

"Love it!" Leeza said. "Now, we're all matching."

"And what about you, Leeza?" Cristal smacked on her deep fried chicken gizzards with rice and gravy. "We were so sorry to hear about your dad...your mom...and all like that—"

"I'm better." Leeza put them at ease. "At first I was so embarrassed, so angry." She admitted. "The idea of my Dad...trying to kill my Mom...to buy me a career...with blood money. It made me furious! I hated him for taking me through this...and for dying before he could help me understand why." A lump rose in her throat. "But Jasmine, here, prayed with me, prayed for me, and talked me through it."

"That was real nice of you, Jasmine." Cristal winked. "And I was praying for y'all, too."

"And then I decided." Leeza continued. "I decided that I love my Mom...I love my Dad. And I was not going to let his choices—as horrible as they were—take over my life. And I wasn't going to let my career—the career he forced me into—rob me of my life."

"Good for you." Cristal nodded.

Leeza dabbed her eyes. "So," she said, "I've gone back to my first love—painting."

"Tell her your news." Jasmine prompted.

"Well, Cristal," Leeza said. "I'd left one of my paintings in a SoHo gallery years ago. I never thought it would sell. But I got a call from the gallery owner the same day I quit my job." She clapped her hands like cymbals. "It sold! It sold!" Leeza rejoiced. "And the buyer is asking for more, which I just happened to have, since that cut-throat job of mine had me so stressed out, I was painting every spare minute."

"You go, Girl!" Cristal raved.

"And my new patron is pushing my work to his rich friends on both coasts." Leeza smiled. "He's planning a show for me in Hollywood in the fall and in Manhattan in the spring."

"Wow!" Cristal and Jasmine exclaimed. "You're on your way!"

"But, Cristal," Leeza said soberly, "none of this would've been possible if you hadn't encouraged Jasmine to call me—"

"Forced me to call you is more like it." Jasmine grinned.

"Jasmine helped me see...and I accepted Jesus Christ as my Saviour and Lord," Leeza said. "And, now, He's leading me into my...true calling. And I'm learning to live...in the seventh day—

"The seventh day?" Cristal put down her fork. "My pastor and my husband, Malik, tried to push that on me—telling me to chill out and let the Lord do the work—"

"But truth be told," Jasmine inserted, "getting to tell Leeza about Jesus helped me, too."

"How so?"

"I'd been dragging some old sins around for years—trying to fix it myself." Jasmine's voice misted over. "But, now, I truly believe Jesus has forgiven me...every one of my sins...and I am totally free—"

"No doubt, Girlfriend." Cristal spouted. "Jesus don't half-do nothing."

"So tell us, Cristal." Jasmine smiled at her friend's straight-shooting style and her uncomplicated faith. "What you been up to, Girl?"

"I got me some babies!" Cristal's gray eyes sparkled. "Well, they're really my sister's four kids, but me and Malik are raising them now 'cause my sister, Chanel...well, she's struggling."

"Why? What happened?"

"Her husband, Denver, left her, and she's having a hard time dealing with it." Cristal shrugged. "It's a long story, but it seems her having all them babies wasn't about love, like I thought. It was about Chanel trying to hold onto her man. And when it didn't work, she kinda fell to pieces."

"Sorry to hear that," Jasmine said.

"No worries." Cristal beamed. "Me and Malik are keeping the kids through the week—loving on 'em; making sure they get to school on time; get their homework; taking 'em to church and stuff like that. And on the weekends, they go over to be with Chantilly and Chanel, so me and Malik can have a little *we* time. It's hectic, but I love them kids, and I'm real happy with everything. Who knew the Lord would use us to raise my own sister's kids, right?" Cristal sighed. "But He had it planned for me all along—"

"But who's Chantilly?" Leeza quizzed.

Cristal smirked. "Oh, she's their Grandmother—"

"Your mother?" Jasmine frowned.

"Yup," Cristal said. "But I don't call her that anymore." She relaxed her shoulders. "She's Chantilly to me."

"But—"

"Long story." Cristal raised her hand. "But let's just say I found out her husband is not my 'biological' father." She flashed air quotes with her polka-dot tips.

"Oh!" Leeza's mouth formed a perfect circle while Jasmine was still getting there. "What!?!"

"But no worries." Cristal beamed. "All is forgiven. We've sorted it all out. The Lord has helped me love her…and my newfound Daddy, too—"

"You found your real daddy?"

"Yup, and he's way-cool," Cristal said seriously. "And Malik and Pastor finally helped me realize that all that stressing I was doing over having a baby had to do with trying to win Chantilly's love. Not knowing that she was withholding her love from me 'cause the guilt she was feeling for cheating on her husband was eating her alive." Cristal snapped her fingers. "But I've got it, now; and I'm really getting into this seventh day stuff."

"Yes, indeed." Jasmine nodded. "There're lots of reasons people don't love us that have absolutely nothing to do with us."

Cristal glimmered. "Well, needless to say, all that madness is over, and she'll be Chantilly to me from here on out."

"Well, I'm glad you were able to let it go," Leeza said. "Because all of us have mixed motives—some we're aware of, and some we're not." She giggled. "And truth be told, ours aren't any better than theirs. So all we can do is forgive each other...and move on."

"Speaking of which," Cristal said brightly, "I might even start-up me a little foundation."

"Foundation?"

"Yeah," Cristal said, "I've got a little money coming to me, see; and I may use it to help couples like me and Malik that's trying to have a baby."

"What would you call it?" Leeza grappled with the business angle.

"I don't know." Cristal mused. "Maybe something like—*So You Wanna Have a Baby?*" She giggled. "But we want to encourage couples to do what they do—try anything and everything—but to wait on the Lord and accept the best plan for their lives."

"Not a bad idea." Jasmine agreed.

Cristal's eyes lit up. "And I have one more little surprise for us in the spirit of moving on—" She signaled the waiter who'd been waiting in the wings. "Ba-Bam!"

"At your service, ma'am." The waiter stepped forward, producing a chilled bottle of champagne and three fluted glasses.

Leeza's jaw dropped. "How did you swing this...at a soul food restaurant?"

Cristal smiled. "You can do just about anything in the ATL if you've got the bucks."

"But I don't drink," Jasmine said.

"You most certainly will drink a toast with this high-priced *Cristal* champagne I ordered." Cristal bristled. "Jesus turned water into wine at the party," she said, "and I'm sure He'll have no problem with us toasting our blessings."

"C'mon, Jasmine." Leeza urged. "It's just one toast." She teared up. "And we truly have been blessed."

"Okay-Okay." Jasmine agreed. "One toast."

On cue, the waiter handed each of them a glass and popped the cork. The expensive champagne bubbled over the sides. He poured the sparkling liquid into Jasmine's glass, then Leeza's glass. But Cristal set her hand atop her glass and refused. Instead, she poured the remains from her water glass into her champagne flute.

"What's this?" Jasmine grumbled. "You force me into a toast, and you're not drinking?"

"But you see...I can't." Cristal grinned from ear to ear. "I'm preg-nant!!"

"Oh, my God!" Their giggles bubbled over and sparkled like the rich champagne. They raised their glasses and clinked them joyfully. "To Living in the Seventh Day!" They proclaimed jubilantly. "Living in the Seventh Day!"

***

*"For he that is entered into His rest,
he also hath ceased from his own works,
as God did from His." Hebrews 4:10*

ABOUT THE AUTHOR

Jeanetta Britt is a bestselling, award-winning author who graduated Magna Cum Laude from Fisk University and finished Top Ten with a Master's degree from The University of Michigan. Her passion for writing contemporary Christian Fiction novels—filled with lots of juicy drama and suspense—as well as, Gospel poetry, surfaced in 1996 and has grown steadily since that time. "While being swept up in the story," Jeanetta says, "I want my readers to *feel* the love of Jesus and take refuge in Him, like I did."

After completing a 30-year career in public administration in Dallas, Texas, Jeanetta returned to her native Alabama to write and to live. Her southern roots are reflected in her imagery, characters, and delightfully witty storytelling style. She is a sought-after inspirational speaker, by youth and adults alike, with six novels and five books of poetry to her credit.

Jeanetta is also an avid gardener and community advocate, and she founded Twelve Stones CDC—a non-profit organization that operates two community gardens in rural Alabama. "We provide free, fresh food for our community and an opportunity for our youth and senior citizens to form that vital intergenerational connection, and to get some free exercise, companionship and sunshine, too," she says. "No rules—just love!"

www.ingramcontent.com/pod-product-compliance
Lightning Source LLC
Chambersburg PA
CBHW060915180626
46817CB00004B/1264